Ancient Buddhist Wisdom

For A Peaceful & Happy Life

Ancient Buddhist Wisdom

For A Peaceful & Happy Life

NAVEEN KUMAR CHANDRA (IAS)

PRABHAT
PRAKASHAN

Published by
PRABHAT PRAKASHAN PVT. LTD.
4/19 Asaf Ali Road,
New Delhi-110 002 (INDIA)
e-mail: prabhatbooks@gmail.com

ISBN 978-93-5562-067-5
ANCIENT BUDDHIST WISDOM
by Naveen Kumar Chandra (IAS)

Edition
First, 2023

Price
₹ 250 (Rupees Two Hundred Fifty Only)

Printed at
Japan Art, Delhi

Dedicated to my family.

Author's Note

Dear Readers,

It is with immense joy and reverence that I present to you "Ancient Buddhist Wisdom." This book is a heartfelt endeavor to bridge the timeless teachings of Lord Buddha with the complexities of modern living, offering you a transformative guide to lead a simpler and more purposeful life.

In crafting "Ancient Buddhist Wisdom," I drew inspiration from the vast treasure trove of Buddhist literature and the profound insights of ancient Buddhist scholars. These teachings, rooted in the enlightened wisdom of Lord Buddha, have withstood the test of time, offering a timeless roadmap to navigate the complexities of existence with grace and compassion.

As we embark on this journey of discovery, we will delve into fundamental Buddhist principles that hold the potential to awaken profound shifts within us. We will explore the essence of impermanence, the boundless wellspring of compassion, the transformative power of mindfulness, and the liberating practice of non-attachment.

In each chapter, you will find the teachings thoughtfully presented in a modern context, allowing you to grasp their essence and relevance in your everyday life. I have endeavored to craft a narrative that resonates with both seasoned practitioners and those new to the path of Buddhism, ensuring that the wisdom conveyed transcends cultural and geographical boundaries.

"Ancient Buddhist Wisdom" is not just a collection of ancient insights; it is an invitation to embark on an inner journey of self-discovery. Each page aims to ignite a spark of inspiration and contemplation, guiding you towards a profound understanding of your own mind and emotions.

I encourage you, dear readers, to read these pages with an open heart and an open mind. Embrace the teachings not merely as intellectual knowledge but as tools for personal growth and transformation. Allow the wisdom of the Buddha to seep into your being, gently guiding you towards a life of greater clarity, compassion, and purpose.

As you read, I invite you to reflect on the timeless truths presented here and consider how they can enrich your daily life. From simple mindfulness practices to cultivating compassion for oneself and others, the wisdom of the Buddha holds the key to unlocking the fullness of your potential.

I am deeply grateful to all the ancient Buddhist scholars, whose timeless words have guided countless seekers throughout history. Their wisdom continues to be a guiding light for those of us navigating the complexities of the modern world.

May "Ancient Buddhist Wisdom" be a cherished companion on your personal quest for inner peace and enlightenment. May it inspire you to embody the spirit of compassion, and may its insights empower you to create a more harmonious and compassionate world for all beings.

With boundless gratitude and warmest regards,

– Naveen Kumar Chandra (IAS)

❑

Acknowledgements

I stand humbled and deeply grateful as I take a moment to express my heartfelt appreciation to all those whose unwavering support and guidance have made "Ancient Buddhist Wisdom" a reality. This book would not have been possible without the collective efforts and encouragement of numerous individuals, each playing a significant role in bringing this work to fruition.

First and foremost, I extend my deepest gratitude to Lord Buddha, the enlightened one, whose timeless teachings form the very foundation of this book. His profound wisdom has guided countless generations, and it is an honor to present these ancient insights to a modern audience seeking a path to inner harmony and fulfillment.

I am immensely thankful to the ancient Buddhist scholars and sages whose writings have paved the way for the dissemination of wisdom across the ages. Their dedication to preserving and sharing the teachings of Lord Buddha has left an indelible mark on humanity's quest for truth and enlightenment.

I extend my heartfelt appreciation to my family, whose unconditional love and support have been a source of strength throughout this journey. Their encouragement and understanding allowed me the space to delve into the vast ocean of Buddhist literature and distill its essence into this book. My father, mother, sisters have all been extremely supportive. My wife's efforts to know and learn more about Buddhism and Buddhist teachings, inspired me to write a book for her on the topic and make Buddhist philosophy and ideas more accessible to her and many others like her.

I owe a special debt of gratitude to my editor and the publishing team, whose expertise and commitment to excellence have helped shape this book into its final form. Your invaluable guidance and dedication have made this endeavor a seamless and rewarding experience.

To the countless readers and seekers of truth who will embark on this journey through the pages of "Ancient Buddhist Wisdom," I offer my deepest appreciation. Your openness and willingness to explore these teachings with sincerity fill my heart with hope and gratitude.

Lastly, I acknowledge the ever-present, boundless compassion of all beings. May the wisdom contained within these pages find resonance in your hearts, inspiring each of you to embrace the path of mindfulness, compassion, and non-attachment, leading to a simpler, better life and a more compassionate world.

❑

Contents

❑

I.

Pain is Inevitable, Suffering is Optional

Suffering is your Choice

Imagine you are thrown in jail in the prime of your youth. You are restless, you have ambitious plans, and you wish to bring about a huge change and inspire your fellow countrymen to overthrow a regime that has been characterised by death, destruction and discrimination of your people. But now that you are in jail and there is no way for you to come out anytime soon, it seems like all your plans will die with you in the jail itself. This is exactly what happened with Nelson Mandela. He spent 27 years in prison as a political prisoner in South Africa. During this time, he faced immense physical and emotional pain, but he chose not to allow that pain to turn into suffering. Instead, he used his time in prison to educate himself, develop his leadership skills, and become a symbol of hope for his people, inspiring them to achieve the unprecedented and went on to become the president of his nation and a symbol of courage and determination the world over.

'Pain is inevitable, suffering is optional' is a phrase that encapsulates a fundamental truth about the human experience. It is a message that can be found throughout history, philosophy, religion and modern psychology. This phrase has been attributed to many different sources, but the concept behind it remains the same: we cannot always control the pain that we experience in life, but we can choose whether or not to allow that pain to turn into suffering.

Stephen Hawking was a renowned physicist who lived with amyotrophic lateral sclerosis (ALS) for most of his life. Despite being confined to a wheelchair and losing the ability to speak, he continued to make groundbreaking contributions to the field of physics and inspire others with his determination and resilience. He never gave up. When almost everyone around him lost hope, he did not. He didn't let his pain turn into suffering. He never let himself become a victim of his condition, instead, he decided to fight till his last breath and he did.

This concept of pain and suffering finds its first mention in the teachings of Buddhism, in the Four Noble truths in Buddhism. The first Noble Truth of Buddhism is that life is characterised by suffering. This does not mean that life is entirely negative or full of pain, but rather that we all experience some form of loss, pain and disappointment. The second Noble Truth of Buddhism is that suffering is caused by our attachment to things that are impermanent, to the material world, to our desires. This attachment leads to craving, which in turn leads to suffering. The third Noble Truth in Buddhism is that suffering can be overcome by letting go of attachment.

This concept of suffering is also dealt with in ancient Hindu religion, where it is linked to the idea of karma. Karma is the law of cause and effect, and it teaches that our actions have consequences. If we act in ways that harm others, we will experience negative consequences in our life or in future lives. If we act in ways that benefit others, we will experience positive consequences. The law of karma, to an extent, gives us control over our pain and suffering. The ultimate goal in Hinduism is to achieve moksha, or liberation from the cycle of birth and death, which can only be achieved by overcoming attachment and achieving self-realisation. Overcoming attachment would mean letting go of any unwanted and unreasonable desire.

This is not an entirely religious or spiritual concept. Scientifically, pain is a necessary aspect of the human experience. Pain is a signal that something is wrong, and it motivates us to take action to address the problem. However, suffering is not a necessary outcome of pain. Suffering occurs when we resist pain, when we feel sorry for ourselves, or when we obsess over our pain. Research in positive psychology has shown that our attitude toward pain has a significant impact on our experience of it. When we accept pain as a natural part of life and focus on the positive aspects of our situation, we are less likely to suffer.

In modern psychology, the concept of suffering is closely linked to the idea of resilience. Resilience is our ability to bounce back from adversity and maintain a positive attitude in the face of difficulty. Resilience is not a fixed trait; it can be developed through practice and experience. One of the key components of resilience is the ability to accept and adapt to change. When we resist change, we create suffering for ourselves. When we accept change and focus on the positive aspects of our situation, we are able to move forward with greater ease.

❑

2
The Mind is Everything

Your thoughts make you

The mind is everything. What you think you become.

—The Buddha

You are raped as a kid and humiliated. You live in the most extreme poverty. You are not even allowed to dream or have any hope. This is exactly what happened to Oprah Winfrey.

Oprah is a media mogul who has achieved great success in her career, so much so that in every US Presidential election, there are rumours of her running for the post and every time there are predictions of her winning the race if she decides to run. She has often spoken about the power of positive thinking and visualisation in her life. She has said, “The biggest adventure you can ever take is to live the life of your dreams.” Oprah’s success is a testament to the power which our mindset has on our lives.

‘The mind is everything. What you think you become’ is a powerful reminder of the importance of our thoughts in shaping our lives. This ancient wisdom from Buddhism plays a very important role in not just the destination we reach but also in our having a satisfying and happy journey. The Buddhist concept of mindfulness emphasises the importance of cultivating a clear and focused mind in order to live in the present moment.

Ancient works, such as the Bhagavad Gita and the *Yoga Sutras* of Patanjali, teach that the mind is the most powerful force in the universe. It is this weapon that we wield to conquer all our fears. It is thus very important to keep this weapon rust-free. The Bhagavad Gita describes the mind as a ‘friend’ or a ‘foe’ depending on how it is trained. It is a friend if it is treated and trained as such and shall come to our aid in time of need. It is a foe if we neglect it. If we think negatively most of the time, it will become our worst enemy. The *Yoga Sutras* don’t just recognise the power of our minds but also offer practices for purifying and controlling the mind. These teachings emphasise the importance of self-awareness, mindfulness, and meditation in cultivating a healthy and powerful mind.

In more recent times, scientific research has shown that the mind and body are interconnected and that our thoughts and emotions can have a powerful impact on our physical health. Studies have found that stress, negative thinking, and emotional suppression can lead to a range of health problems, including cardiovascular disease, diabetes and cancer. On the other hand, positive thinking, gratitude, and emotional expression have been shown to improve health outcomes and overall well-being.

Modern psychology has also explored the power of the mind in shaping our experiences. Cognitive-behavioural therapy (CBT), for example, is a widely used therapy that helps individuals identify and change negative thought patterns that contribute to mental health issues such as anxiety and depression. CBT and other therapies emphasise the importance of our thoughts in shaping our emotions and behaviours, and offer tools for cultivating a more positive and constructive mindset.

Philosophers, new and old, have also explored the power of the mind in shaping our lives. The Stoics, for example, emphasised the importance of cultivating a mindset of resilience and self-control in order to overcome challenges and live a fulfilling life.

'What you think you become' speaks of the fundamental importance of our thoughts in shaping our lives. By becoming more aware of our thoughts and working to cultivate a positive and resilient mindset, we can create the life we want to live and make a positive impact in the world. "We are shaped by our thoughts; we become what we think. When the mind is pure, joy follows like a shadow that never leaves."

❑

3
Peace Comes from Within

Inner peace does not come externally

Peace comes from within. Do not seek it without.

— The Buddha

'Peace comes from within. Do not seek it without' has been attributed to the Buddha, and it reflects a central teaching of many spiritual traditions and has been embraced by all great teachers who followed after him in all traditions, all over the world.

'Peace comes from within', means that true peace and contentment cannot be found in external circumstances or material possessions. Instead, they must come from within us. This is a common theme in many spiritual traditions, which emphasise the importance of inner cultivation and spiritual practices such as meditation and mindfulness. While 'Do not seek it without', means that we should not look for peace outside of ourselves. This is a powerful reminder that we are the source of our own happiness and well-being. While external factors can certainly affect our state of mind, ultimately, our happiness is under our own control.

Ancient works such as the Bhagavad Gita and the *Tao Te Ching* contain similar teachings about the importance of inner cultivation and the pursuit of inner peace. In the Bhagavad Gita, for example, Lord Krishna teaches Arjuna that true wisdom and happiness come from within and that the self is the ultimate source of peace and contentment. This idea now has the backing of several research findings and studies done at various universities. Studies have shown that meditation and mindfulness practices can reduce stress, improve mood, and enhance overall health and well-being.

Modern psychology has also explored the concept of inner peace and its relationship to mental health. The field of positive psychology, for example, emphasises the importance of cultivating positive emotions such as gratitude and compassion, in order to enhance overall well-being. It is important to cultivate positive emotions as they are the guides in our search for inner peace; they make us look inwards, inside our souls.

Stoic philosophers have also emphasised the importance of inner peace and the ability to control one's own thoughts and emotions. Marcus Aurelius, the famous Stoic philosopher and Roman emperor, wrote in his *Meditations*: "You have power over your mind, not outside events. Realise this, and you will find strength."

Mahatma Gandhi advocated for nonviolent resistance and was opposed to any kind of violence in India's freedom struggle. This principle was also based on the importance he gave to inner peace as a means of achieving social and political change. He famously said, "Be the change you wish to see in the world." His commitment to inner peace and nonviolence helped to inspire a movement that led to the independence of India.

High-achieving athletes who are able to stay calm and focused under pressure often perform at their best. Tennis player Novak Djokovic, winner of the most singles Grand Slams in men's tennis history, for example, has spoken about the importance of mental training and meditation in his success on the court. He speaks about how it is important to find peace within before you conquer the world outside.

'Peace comes from within. Do not seek it without', reflects a universal truth. By cultivating inner peace through spiritual practices, positive emotions, and the ability to control our thoughts and emotions, we can enhance our well-being and make a positive impact on the world.

❑

4
One Word that Brings Peace

Speak less, listen more

Better than a thousand hollow words, is one word that brings peace.

—The Buddha

'Better than a thousand hollow words, is one word that brings peace' is a powerful reminder of the importance of speaking with intention and mindfulness. This quote has been attributed to the Buddha, and it reflects a central teaching of many spiritual traditions.

Ancient works such as the *Tao Te Ching* contain similar teachings about the importance of mindful and purposeful speech. In the *Tao Te Ching*, for example, Lao Tzu writes: "The wise speak because they have something to say; fools speak because they have to say something." This is a reminder of the importance of speaking with intention and mindfulness. It is not just limited to spoken words but actions as well.

Words have a powerful impact on our well-being and the world around us. Studies have shown that positive words and expressions of gratitude can improve our mood and well-being, while negative words can have the opposite effect. At the same time, negative words or negative expressions affect our mindset, affect people around us, and can get us into a lot of unnecessary trouble.

Human psychology has also explored the concept of the impact of our spoken words on our well-being. Many findings emphasise the importance of using positive language to enhance our well-being and improve our relationships with others. Positive language and reinforcement can have a long-lasting impact on our mental health. Many studies also suggest that we speak out loud with ourselves, affirming positive statements.

Philosophers such as Aristotle have also emphasised the importance of speaking with intention and purpose. He wrote in his *Nicomachean Ethics*: "It is the mark of an educated mind to be able to entertain a thought without accepting it." This emphasises the importance of considering our words before speaking and using them to convey ideas with meaning and purpose. In the times that we live in, where there is too much of everything, more so, too much content, it is imperative for us to understand the value of less when it comes to our words.

'Better than a thousand hollow words, is one word that brings peace' is a reminder of the power of words to impact our well-being and the world around us. By speaking with intention and mindfulness, we can use our words to inspire and uplift others and promote peace and unity. It is also a reminder that if we don't have anything of use to say, it is much better to listen than speak unnecessarily and without purpose.

❑

5
Love What You Do

When play is work, work becomes play.

The only way to do great work is to love what you do.
—Steve Jobs

'The only way to do great work is to love what you do'—this quote by Steve Jobs highlights the importance of having passion for one's work. Many successful people in various fields have attributed their success to their love for what they do.

The Bhagavad Gita, one of the most important Hindu scriptures, emphasises the importance of performing one's duty with passion and devotion. The concept of karma yoga, which is the path of selfless action, teaches that performing deeds without attachment to the outcome leads to inner peace and spiritual growth. We should be selfless and not just mechanically go through life, but also love what we do. When we love what we do and do what we love, only then can we realise our full potential.

The famous Chinese philosopher Confucius believed that work is a noble pursuit and that one should find joy and satisfaction in one's work. He said, "Choose a job you love, and you will never have to work a day in your life." One needs to find satisfaction in any work they do. To begin with, one should be passionate about the work they do. It should excite them, and make them look forward to each day.

One of the most well-known examples of someone who loved what they did is Steve Jobs, co-founder of Apple Inc. Jobs once said, "Your work is going to fill a large part of your life, and the only way to be truly satisfied is to do what you believe is great work. And the only way to do great work is to love what you do." His philosophy of loving his work made him come up with products and ideas which have revolutionised multiple industries. His passion for technology, eye for detail, and perfectionism in pursuit of a mission made him deliver some of the most iconic products ever.

Multiple studies have shown that individuals who are passionate about their work, experience higher levels of job satisfaction and are more likely to achieve success. Passion for one's work can lead to increased creativity, productivity and motivation. It is thus not just in the interests of our material well-being but also our health, both mental and physical, that we try and find where our passion is. Many psychologists suggest that individuals who find meaning and purpose in their work are more likely to be engaged and satisfied with their jobs. Finding meaning in one's work can lead to a sense of fulfillment, and greater overall well-being.

Philosopher Friedrich Nietzsche believed that the key to happiness is to find something to do that gives one a sense of purpose and meaning. He said, "He who has a why to live for can bear almost any how."

Michael Jordan, considered one of the greatest basketball players of all time, was known for his love of the game. He once said, "I play to win, whether during practice or a real game. And I will not let anything get in the way of me and my competitive enthusiasm to win." It is this enthusiasm for what we do, it is this love for what we do that makes us achieve greatness. Even if we don't reach the lofty heights of a Michael Jordan, we would still find happiness.

Loving what you do is essential for achieving success and fulfillment in life. It allows for creativity, motivation and a sense of purpose. Whether in work, hobbies or relationships, finding something that you love and are passionate about can lead to a more meaningful and satisfying life. Remember, 'The only way to do great work is to love what you do'.

❑

6

Hatred does not Cease by Hatred

Love wins, always.

Hatred does not cease by hatred, but only by love;
this is the eternal rule.

– The Buddha

This powerful statement speaks of the importance of compassion and empathy in our lives. It is a quote that has been passed down through the ages, and is present in many different traditions and cultures. This quote teaches us that the only way to overcome hatred and anger is by love and understanding.

In Buddhism, this quote is attributed to the Buddha. In the Dhammapada, one of the Buddhist scriptures, the Buddha said,

"Hatred does not cease by hatred; hatred ceases by love alone. This is an eternal law." This has since been almost a universal law, inspiring scores of leaders in their struggles, motivating people to fight their worst enemies, lifting people when they have been down and out, but at the same time making them understand the difference between sin and the sinner. Mahatma Gandhi, for example, used nonviolent resistance to fight for India's independence from British colonial rule. He believed that responding to violence with violence would only lead to more violence and suffering and that the only way to truly overcome the British was by love and understanding.

Another great example where this principle worked as a miracle comes from the life of Nelson Mandela. He also exemplified this idea in his fight against apartheid in South Africa. Despite spending 27 years in prison, Mandela never lost sight of the importance of forgiveness and reconciliation. He believed that the only way to overcome the legacy of apartheid was through love and understanding, and so when he was released, he did not harbour thoughts of revenge but reconciliation.

In ancient Hinduism, the idea of responding to hatred with love is from the Bhagavad Gita. Chapter 16, Verse 3, states how, perplexed by various anxieties and bounded by a network of illusions, people become attached to the enjoyment of the senses and fall into hell. People do not just rejoice in others' successes but also their failures, thus bringing about their downfall.

Not just religious scriptures, but scientific research also has shown that practicing empathy and compassion can have a positive impact on our physical and mental health. In a study published in *Journal of Social and Clinical Psychology*, researchers found that people who practiced loving-kindness meditation, a type of meditation that focuses on generating feelings of love and compassion towards oneself and others, experienced a decrease in the symptoms of anxiety and depression. Additionally, the study found that participants who practiced loving-kindness meditation were more likely to engage in prosocial behavior, such as helping others. It goes without saying that love is the most potent weapon in our fight against hate. Hate breeds more hatred and the vicious cycle continues.

In modern psychology, positive psychology advocates responding to hatred with love. Positive psychology is a branch of psychology that focuses on promoting well-being and happiness. One of the guiding principles of positive psychology is the idea of cultivating positive emotions, such as love, gratitude and compassion. By cultivating these positive emotions, we can improve our overall sense of well-being and happiness.

"Hatred does not cease by hatred, but only by love; this is the eternal rule," is a powerful statement that reminds us of the importance of responding to hatred and anger with love and understanding. Not only world leaders and politicians, everyone, every human being should let go of hate. Keeping hate and anger inside kills us first.

❑

7
Three Things Cannot be Long Hidden

Truth shall always come out.

Three things cannot be long hidden: the sun, the moon, and the truth.

— The Buddha

Hiding the truth is not sustainable in the long run; not just not sustainable but not possible. Honesty and integrity are thus not choices we make to live a better life. We have no choice if we wish to live our lives well.

This quote reminds us that no matter how hard we try to hide the truth, it will eventually come to light. This is because the truth is a fundamental aspect of our existence that cannot be ignored or denied. It can't be held back, hidden, broken and distorted, and even if it is, not for long. Truth is just like the sun and the moon, it may be eclipsed for a while but it will come out of the eclipse. Truth is a force of nature that cannot be altered or changed. It is a part of the natural order of things, and as such, cannot be hidden or suppressed for long. Nature does not lie and it is thus just a waste for us to indulge in it. It is unnatural for us to do so, and that is why when we do, we are always sure, even in our own selves, of the suffering and pain it brings to everyone.

The quote also emphasizes the importance of honesty and integrity in our lives. When we try to hide the truth or deceive others, we are going against the natural order. We act in a way that is contrary to the truth, and this can have negative consequences for ourselves and others. By embracing honesty and integrity, we are aligning ourselves with the truth and living in a way that is in harmony with the natural order of things.

Living truthfully although sufficient for its sake, also has many benefits for ourselves and for those around us. When we are honest with ourselves and others, we earn the trust and respect of others. We are seen as reliable or dependable, and people are more likely to trust us with important tasks and responsibilities. Additionally, when we live truthfully, we are more at peace with ourselves. We don't have to worry about keeping up with lies or being found out, and we can focus on living our lives in a way that is authentic and true to ourselves.

One of the most important lessons we can learn from the quote is the importance of being true to ourselves. When we are honest with ourselves, we are better able to understand our thoughts, feelings and motivations. This self-awareness allows us to live in a way that is authentic and true to ourselves, and it helps us to make decisions that are in line with our values and beliefs. This way we avoid any internal conflicts; we avoid going against our values; we avoid ethical dilemmas; we avoid finding ourselves stuck and unable to take any decision all the time.

Another lesson we learn from the quote is the importance of taking responsibility for our actions. When we try to hide the truth or deceive others, we are avoiding responsibility for our actions. This can lead to feelings of guilt and shame, and it can damage our relationships with others. By taking responsibility for our actions and being honest about our mistakes, we show that we are willing to learn and grow, and we can build stronger relationships with those around us.

By embracing honesty and living truthfully, we can build trust and respect, live authentically, and make decisions that are in line with our values and beliefs. We can also take responsibility for our actions and build stronger relationships with those around us. This quote serves as a powerful reminder that the truth will always come to light, and that living truthfully is the only sustainable way to live our lives.

❑

8

Do not Dwell in the Past

Live in the moment.

Do not dwell in the past, do not dream of the future, concentrate the mind on the present moment.

— The Buddha

Many of us often find ourselves dwelling on the past, regretting our mistakes, and thinking about events and how their courses could've been different only if we did that or didn't do this. We worry about the future, thinking far too ahead, or worry about things so distant in the future that it is almost impossible to know how things could be. We forget to live in the present moment, the only time that truly exists and the only moment we can control. It is true that our present is shaped by our actions in the past, but only to a certain extent. How we deal with it, and what we make of it, is all still in our hands. We dwell on the past or worry about the future and ignore the only thing we can change. However, the ancient wisdom of various cultures suggests that focusing on the present moment is not just beneficial for the best possible use of the limited time we have, but can improve our mental health and overall well-being.

The concept of living in the present moment can be traced back to ancient Buddhist teachings. The Buddha emphasized the importance of mindfulness, or being fully present and aware in the current moment. The practice of mindfulness involves observing our thoughts, feelings and sensations without judgment, and bringing our attention back to the present moment whenever our mind starts to wander. This practice has been shown to reduce stress, anxiety and depression, and improve overall well-being. Being in the present moment is not just about accepting the present, but being aware of it. Awareness goes beyond knowing; it goes beyond just seeing; it goes beyond just hearing; it is about embracing the present moment with all that we've got.

Recent scientific studies have also supported the benefits of mindfulness. A study published in *Journal of Personality and Social Psychology* found that individuals who practice mindfulness are less likely to be caught up in worries and negative thoughts about the future or the past. Another study conducted at Harvard Medical School found that mindfulness meditation can lead to changes in the brain that improve attention, empathy and emotional regulation.

In modern Western psychology, mindfulness-based cognitive therapy (MBCT) has been developed as a treatment for depression and anxiety. MBCT combines mindfulness practices with cognitive therapy to help individuals become more aware of their thoughts and emotions, and learn to respond to them more constructively. Studies have shown that MBCT can be as effective as medication for preventing depression relapse.

Steve Jobs, the founder of Apple, said, "If you are focused on the past or the future, you can't be in the present, and therefore you'll miss so much." What he meant was though future vision might be necessary to guide you, to put you on a path, to obsess over it, and forget the things you need to do now to get to that future, won't help you.

Eckhart Tolle, a spiritual teacher and author, wrote extensively on the concept of mindfulness and being present in the moment. He believes that the present moment is the only place where we can experience true happiness and fulfilment. He also says that worrying about future happiness or past sadness and making the present unpleasant is like robbing yourself. You are harming yourself.

'Do not dwell in the past, do not dream of the future, concentrate the mind on the present moment' is a reminder that the present moment is the only time that truly exists. By focusing on the present moment, we can reduce stress and anxiety, improve our mental health and overall well-being, and experience true happiness and fulfilment. The ancient wisdom of mindfulness, supported by modern scientific research and psychology, has shown that being present in the moment can have profound benefits for our lives. It must be remembered that the past is gone, nothing ever changes the past and the future is not yet here and anything small or big can change it completely, so it's only logical to focus on this very moment.

❑

9
Rise Up and be Thankful

Be thankful, be grateful.

Let us rise up and be thankful, for if we didn't learn a lot today, at least we learned a little, and if we didn't learn a little, at least we didn't get sick, and if we got sick, at least we didn't die; so, let us all be thankful

— The Buddha

These are the wise words of the Buddha, reminding us to appreciate what we have and find reasons to be grateful for even the seemingly small things in life. This quote is a beautiful reminder of the power of gratitude and how it can shift our mindset from one of lack, to one of abundance. It reminds us of the fact that what we have and take for granted is perhaps everything to someone; what we have and don't bother about would mean the world to many people. It reminds us that we should always be grateful for what we have and be thankful for all that we possess.

Gratitude isn't just a spiritual term but it has been studied extensively in the field of positive psychology and has been found to have numerous benefits for our mental and physical health. In fact, studies have shown that people who regularly practice gratitude are happier, more optimistic, and experience less stress and depression. Additionally, people who practice gratitude have been found to have stronger immune systems, better sleep, and even live longer. What do we mean by practicing gratitude? What we mean is that, for example, if you have a tough boss at your workplace, you feel that your boss is not fair and maybe mistreats you, practicing gratitude in this situation would mean that you understand and appreciate, and acknowledge that there are many people, much more talented, much more qualified who would do anything to get your job. Practicing gratitude would mean that you should not start hating your work or disliking your job. You must understand that a tough boss does not mean a bad job. You have to deal with it in such a way that it doesn't make you a bitter person. You have to see and try to figure out why it is that your boss is unreasonable. If it is something you can change, do it; if it is something you can't, tell them. After all this, if they still treat you miserably, you should quietly look for other options, but at the same time develop no ill-will towards your boss, your job or your colleagues. Remember, this job paid your bills, taught you a lot, and supported you. If it was a difficult work environment, you still learnt how to work in a stressful and challenging environment. Just be grateful and move on with peace.

One of the reasons why gratitude is so powerful is that it helps us shift our focus from what we lack to what we have. When we take time to appreciate what we have, we start to see our lives in a different light. We realize that we have much to be thankful for, even in the midst of challenging situations. This shift in perspective can help us feel more positive and optimistic, even during difficult times.

Tony Robbins, the famous teacher, guru and spiritual leader, has emphasized the importance of gratitude in his teachings, encouraging people to find reasons to be thankful even in challenging situations. It is one of the ways to help us keep going and keep moving. Smiling in the face of adversity means we are not giving up. We are facing it and we are looking over and beyond.

The idea of being thankful for what we have is not a new concept. In fact, it is deeply rooted in many ancient wisdom traditions. The Stoics, for example, emphasized the importance of gratitude in their philosophy, teaching that we should focus on what we have, rather than what we lack. The ancient Egyptians also believed in the power of gratitude, worshipping the goddess Ma'at representing the virtues of gratitude and balance in the universe.

Oprah Winfrey, for example, has spoken frequently about the power of gratitude and how it has helped her stay grounded and positive throughout her career.

When we practice gratitude, not only do we feel better ourselves, but we also have the power to have a positive impact on the people around us. When we express gratitude to others, we help them feel valued and appreciated, which can help strengthen our relationships and improve our overall well-being.

These words of the Buddha remind us to appreciate what we have and find reasons to be thankful even in challenging situations. Gratitude is a deeply rooted concept and its importance emphasized by many successful people in modern times and ancient times. By practicing gratitude, we can shift our focus from what we lack to what we have, and positively impact those around us. Thus not only do we make the world a better place for ourselves but for others as well.

❑

IO

The Root of Suffering is Attachment

Detachment is key.

The root of suffering is attachment.

— The Buddha

Steve Jobs, once famously said, "Remembering that I'll be dead soon is the most important tool I've ever encountered to help me make the big choices in life." This quote shows that Jobs recognized the impermanence of life and the importance of letting go of attachment to find fulfillment.

The idea that the root of suffering is attachment is a fundamental concept in many spiritual traditions, including

Buddhism, Hinduism and Taoism. This idea has been echoed in modern psychology and philosophy as well.

The concept of attachment and its relation to suffering can be traced back to ancient Eastern philosophy. Buddhism, for instance, teaches that the root of suffering is craving, which arises from attachment. The Buddha taught that attachment to material possessions, relationships, and even our thoughts and ideas leads to suffering. This is because attachment creates a desire to hold onto things, which in turn causes us to suffer when we are inevitably separated from them. This realisation about attachments and desires led Buddha to renounce his worldly possessions and attachments to go on to the search for enlightenment and overcome suffering.

The Hindu concept of attachment is similar, but it is called '*raga*'. In Hinduism, attachment is seen as a source of pain and suffering, as it creates a false sense of security and leads to disappointment when that attachment is lost or threatened.

Taoism, too, emphasizes the importance of non-attachment. The *Tao Te Ching* teaches that the sage does not cling to possessions or desire fame and fortune. Instead, the sage is content with what they have and finds peace in living in harmony with the natural world.

Mahatma Gandhi, the man who led India's freedom struggle, practiced non-attachment and believed that the root of suffering was the attachment to material possessions and desires. He taught us that by practicing non-attachment, we can overcome our ego and find inner peace.

The Greek philosopher Epictetus, for instance, taught that we should focus on what is within our control and let go of what is not. He believed the key to happiness is accepting what we cannot control and focusing on our thoughts and actions.

Modern psychology supports the idea that attachment can lead to suffering. Attachment Theory, developed by British psychologist John Bowlby, suggests that early attachment to caregivers shapes our attachment styles throughout life. These attachment styles can influence our relationships and emotional well-being.

Attachment anxiety, for example, can cause individuals to become overly attached and fearful of losing their partner, leading to feelings of jealousy and insecurity. Attachment avoidance, on the other hand, can cause individuals to avoid closeness and intimacy, leading to feelings of loneliness and isolation.

Studies have also shown that attachment to material possessions can lead to decreased well-being. Materialism, or the desire for material possessions, has been linked to lower levels of life satisfaction, happiness, and psychological well-being.

In philosophy, the concept of attachment is often discussed in relation to the idea of impermanence. Everything in life is impermanent, and attachment to things that are bound to change or fade away will inevitably lead to suffering. One needs to understand and appreciate this fundamental truth of life; nothing lasts forever.

The concept that the root of suffering is attachment is a fundamental idea in many spiritual traditions, as well as in psychology and philosophy. Attachment can lead to suffering—is supported by scientific research and can be seen in the lives of many famous individuals.

❑

II

Nothing Remains without Change

Only change is permanent.

Everything changes, nothing remains without change.

— The Buddha

The Stoic philosopher Epictetus emphasized the importance of distinguishing between things we can control and those we cannot control and accepting the things we cannot change.

In history, we can see examples of the consequences of resisting change. Societies that cling to outdated traditions and resist change often suffer as a result. On the other hand, those that embrace change and adapt to new circumstances thrive and grow.

This profound statement is a reminder that the world is in a constant state of flux and that nothing remains the same forever. Whether it is the seasons changing, the growth and decay of living beings, or the shifting tides of history, change is an inevitable part of life. Understanding and accepting this fact can help us cope with the challenges of life and adapt to new circumstances. Even if we were to remain still, and not do anything, the world moves on; time moves on.

Ancient works and wisdom from various cultures have highlighted the inevitability of change. In Buddhism, the concept of impermanence (*anitya*) is a fundamental principle that everything in the universe is constantly changing. *Anitya*, which translates to impermanence, is the idea that all things, both tangible and intangible, are constantly changing and are therefore impermanent. This includes material possessions, relationships, emotions, and even thoughts.

To overcome this attachment and achieve a state of inner peace, Buddhists strive to cultivate a deep understanding of impermanence. By acknowledging that everything is constantly changing, individuals can learn to let go of attachments and appreciate the present moment.

The concept of *anitya* also plays a role in Buddhist meditation practices. In mindfulness meditation, practitioners focus on their breath and bodily sensations in the present moment. By doing so, they can learn to observe their thoughts and emotions without becoming attached to them. Through consistent practice, individuals can gain a greater understanding of the impermanent nature of thoughts and emotions and reduce their attachment to them.

Additionally, *anitya* is closely tied to the Buddhist concept of dependent origination, or the idea that all things are interconnected and arise from causes and conditions. By understanding this interconnectedness, individuals can cultivate compassion and empathy for all living beings.

This means that we never see the same world ever again, like the famous saying goes, 'You never step in the same water twice'.

The ancient Greek philosopher Heraclitus famously stated, "The only constant in life is change." It means that rather than wasting time over change and worrying about them, it is better to accept and embrace change and learn to adapt to them.

The laws of physics dictate that everything is in a state of constant motion, with atoms and molecules vibrating and moving. Even seemingly solid objects are made up of constantly moving particles. The laws of thermodynamics say that entropy or the disorder in the universe always increases no matter what we do. Our very existence as human beings is a result of small changes that have taken place over millions of years. The process of evolution is driven by the changes in the genetic makeup of living beings over time.

Psychology and philosophy also recognize the importance of understanding and accepting change. The practice of mindfulness teaches us to accept things as they are, rather than resisting or trying to control them.

The Taoist philosophy of Yin and Yang also emphasizes the cyclical nature of change and the need to find balance in a constantly shifting world. It is based on the importance of keeping and understanding balance in the universe, a balance which comes from constant change.

Famous people throughout history have also recognized the importance of embracing change. Steve Jobs famously said, "Innovation distinguishes between a leader and a follower." Jobs understood the importance of constantly innovating and adapting to new technologies and changing consumer needs. He embraced change and used it to revolutionize the technology industry. His philosophy of recognising new trends, and accepting challenges and innovations to come up with radical new products changed the world as we know it.

Mahatma Gandhi, the Indian freedom fighter and spiritual leader, understood that change was necessary to achieve social and political progress. He once said, "You must be the change you wish to see in the world." By leading by example and embracing change, Gandhi was able to inspire others and bring about lasting change in Indian society. This is yet another perspective on change. Here he is not only accepting and embracing change but also urging us to use it as a positive.

Almost all great athletes, without exception, constantly adapt to changes in their opponents' strategies, as well as changes in the rules and equipment of their sport. Those who are able to adapt and innovate often find the most success. Those who are too rigid to change with time are left behind.

The statement 'Everything changes, nothing remains without change' is a reminder that change is an inevitable part of life. Ancient works, scientific research, psychology, philosophy, and examples from history and sports all highlight the importance of understanding and accepting change. By embracing change and adapting to new circumstances, we can navigate through the challenges of life and find success and fulfillment.

❑

12

The Tongue Like a Sharp Knife...

The tongue is a double-edged sword.

The tongue like a sharp knife… kills without drawing blood.

— The Buddha

The tongue is a powerful tool. It can either uplift or destroy a person. It is a double-edged sword that can either bring harmony or chaos.

In many cultures, people believe in the power of words. Words have the power to shape our reality and create the life we desire. Many ancient spiritual teachings have emphasized the importance of the spoken word. For instance, the Bible teaches: "In the beginning was the Word, and the Word was with God, and the Word was God (John 1:1)."

This quote is from the opening verses of the Gospel of John in the Christian Bible. It is a powerful statement about the divine nature of language and the spoken word.

The quote suggests that language has a divine origin and holds a special power in the world. This idea is supported by many ancient traditions and wisdom teachings from around the world. For example, in Hinduism, the concept of 'Nada Brahma' or 'the sound of the universe' suggests that everything in existence is made up of sound vibrations.

Similarly, in the ancient Chinese philosophy of Taoism, the concept of 'the Tao' or 'the way' is seen as a force that underlies and permeates all of existence, and can be accessed through the power of language and words.

The power of language has also been studied and documented by modern science. Research has shown that the words we use have a profound impact on our thoughts, emotions and behaviours. Studies have shown that using positive language can improve our mood, increase our motivation, and even enhance our physical health.

On the other hand, negative language can have a harmful effect on our mental and physical well-being. Research has linked negative self-talk to depression, anxiety, and even physical pain.

The quote also suggests that words have the power to create reality. This idea is explored in depth in the field of linguistics, which studies the relationship between language and the world around us. Linguists have found that the words we use to describe the world can shape our perceptions and beliefs about reality.

For example, the way we talk about a problem can influence our ability to solve it. If we describe a problem as unsolvable or impossible, we may be less likely to find a solution. However, if we approach the same problem with a positive and creative mindset, we may be more likely to find a way forward.

The quote also highlights the potential danger of language. Words have the power to harm and hurt others, even if they don't leave physical scars. This is especially true in today's world, where social media and online communication have made it easier than ever to spread hurtful and damaging words.

It is important to remember that our words have the power to build up or tear down. We must use them wisely and with compassion, knowing that even the most innocent word has the potential to have a profound impact on those around us.

In Buddhism, the right use of speech is one of the practices of the Eightfold Path to enlightenment. In Hinduism, there is another concept, that of 'mantra', where repeating certain words or phrases can bring peace and calmness to the mind.

Scientific research also shows that words have an impact on our brains and behaviour. The words we hear and say can change our brain chemistry and affect our emotions. Studies have shown that positive words and phrases can increase motivation, resilience and overall well-being, while negative words and phrases can increase stress, anxiety and depression.

Furthermore, psychology emphasizes the power of words in shaping our relationships. Words can either build or destroy relationships. The way we communicate with our loved ones, colleagues, and even strangers can either create harmony or conflict. This is why it is essential to choose our words carefully, especially when we are angry or frustrated.

The impact of words is not only limited to our personal lives but also extends to the society we live in. Politicians, leaders and public figures have used words to influence the masses and shape the course of history. Famous speeches like Martin Luther King Jr.'s 'I have a dream' or Nelson Mandela's 'I am the captain of my soul' have inspired millions of people and changed the world.

On the other hand, hate speech, propaganda, and false information can lead to chaos and destruction. The use of words to incite violence and spread hate has caused countless wars and conflicts throughout history.

Moreover, the power of words can be seen in the world of sports. Athletes use affirmations and positive self-talk to enhance their performance and achieve their goals. Muhammad Ali famously said, "I am the greatest" and went on to become one of the greatest boxers in history. Serena Williams has often spoken about the power of positive self-talk and how it has helped her overcome challenges and achieve success.

Words can shape our reality, impact our relationships, and influence the society we live in. It is crucial to choose our words carefully, speak with kindness, and use our words to inspire, uplift, and create harmony.

❑

13

There is no Fire Like Passion

Greed burns everything down.

There is no fire like passion, there is no shark like hatred, there is no snare like folly, there is no torrent like greed.

—The Buddha

The quote comes from the ancient Buddhist text, the Dhammapada. It speaks of the dangers of our intense emotions, which can be likened to destructive forces that can derail us from living fulfilling lives.

Passion, for instance, is often seen as a positive emotion that drives us towards our goals. However, when it is not kept in check, it can become an all-consuming fire that consumes us. We can become so focused on our desires that we lose sight of everything else, including our values, relationships and well-being.

Similarly, hatred can be a powerful emotion that can drive us to harm others, whether through words or actions. It is a destructive force that can tear apart relationships and communities. We may believe that we are justified in our anger and resentment, but ultimately, it only leads to more suffering. Hatred towards anything, no matter how bad or unethical, can never be the right motivation to work and fight against. This negative emotion can never be the solid foundation to build a struggle in which we expect to succeed.

Folly, or foolishness, can also be a snare that traps us in unwise decisions and behaviours. It can cause us to act impulsively, without thinking about the consequences. We may make decisions based on fear, ego, or a desire for instant gratification, instead of considering the long-term effects on ourselves and others.

Finally, greed is like a torrent that can sweep us away in its current. We can become so focused on accumulating wealth, possessions and status that we forget about the things that truly matter in life. We may even engage in unethical behaviour to get what we want, damaging our integrity and reputation in the process. Greed blinds us, we no longer concern ourselves with right or wrong, good or bad; we only wish for more and more. More than we need, more than we can ever need, nothing is enough when we are blinded by greed. We no longer care for our values; we are no longer concerned about the damage we do to ourselves and the people around us. We don't bother about taking what is not rightfully ours and depriving someone else of their rights.

So how can we avoid these destructive forces and find a more balanced, fulfilling way of life? Ancient wisdom and modern research suggest that cultivating mindfulness, self-awareness, and compassion can be powerful antidotes.

Mindfulness, the practice of paying attention to the present moment without judgment, can help us become more aware of our emotions and the ways in which they can influence our behaviour. By observing our thoughts and feelings, we can learn to identify when we are being driven by passion, hatred, folly or greed. With this awareness, we can choose to respond more skillfully, rather than reacting impulsively.

Self-awareness, or the ability to reflect on our own thoughts, feelings and behaviours, is also key to breaking free from destructive patterns. By examining our motivations and values, we can become more intentional about our choices and behaviours. We can also identify the areas where we may be vulnerable to these destructive forces, and take steps to strengthen our resilience and self-control.

Compassion, or the ability to empathize with and care for others, can also be a powerful force in countering destructive emotions. When we are focused on the needs and well-being of others, we are less likely to be consumed by our desires or resentments. We can also cultivate a sense of interconnectedness and common humanity, which can help us to overcome the divisive and destructive forces of hatred and greed.

By becoming more aware of our patterns and motivations, and by focusing on the needs and well-being of others, we can break free from these destructive forces and live more fulfilling, meaningful lives.

❑

14

Believe Nothing

Never follow blindly.

Believe nothing, no matter where you read it or who has said it, not even if I have said it, unless it agrees with your own reason and your own common sense.

— The Buddha

This quote is attributed to Siddhartha Gautama, the founder of Buddhism, whom we know as Lord Buddha. It is a powerful reminder of the importance of critical thinking and individual discernment in a world where we are bombarded with information and opinions from a multitude of sources. Many of the teachings of the Buddha emphasize the importance of relying on one's own discernment when evaluating information and beliefs. The Buddha encouraged his followers to question his teachings and test them against their own experiences and reasoning. He famously stated, "Do not accept what you hear by report, do not accept tradition, do not accept a statement because it is found in our books, nor because it is in accord with your belief, nor because it is the saying of your teacher. Be lamps unto yourselves. Those who, either now or after I am dead, shall rely upon themselves only and not look for assistance to anyone besides themselves, it is they who shall reach the topmost height."

This has become so much more important in the times we live in; in the world we exist today. In a world that is in the middle of a flood of new information on every possible subject, every second. In a world in which we do not know which source to trust and which to ignore, the use of one's own mind and making efforts have become even more important. Misinformation has become a pervasive problem in the modern world, with the rise of social media and other digital platforms. It is increasingly difficult to distinguish truth from falsehood, and this can have serious consequences for individuals, organizations, and society as a whole. One of the challenges of misinformation is that it can spread quickly and easily through digital channels. False information can be shared on social media platforms, blogs, and other websites, and it can be difficult to track down the original source of the information. This can make it challenging for individuals to verify the accuracy of information they encounter online. Misinformation can have serious consequences for individuals, organizations, and society as a whole. For example, false information about medical treatments or health risks can lead to individuals making poor health decisions, which can have serious consequences for their health and well-being. Misinformation can also contribute to social and political unrest, as people may be misled about the actions and intentions of others.

But it is not to say that this is a new problem or that if the digital world becomes more sanitized, we won't need to develop our own independent thinking. Scientific research also supports the idea that critical thinking and individual discernment are essential for making informed decisions. A study published in the *Journal of Applied Research in Memory and Cognition* found that people tend to rely on external sources of information, such as the internet, even when they possess relevant knowledge on a particular topic. The study suggests that people may be more susceptible to misinformation when they fail to utilize their own reasoning and judgment.

Psychology offers insights into why people may be hesitant to trust their own reasoning. The phenomenon known as cognitive dissonance refers to the discomfort people experience when their beliefs and behaviours are inconsistent. In order to reduce this discomfort, people may engage in confirmation bias, seeking out information that confirms their existing beliefs and disregarding information that contradicts them. Overcoming this tendency requires a willingness to challenge one's own beliefs and engage in critical thinking.

Galileo Galilei challenged the widely held belief that Earth was the center of the universe and was ultimately persecuted by the Catholic church for his views. However, his work laid the foundation for modern astronomy and physics. Similarly, Rosa Parks challenged the unjust laws of segregation in the American South and became a symbol of the civil rights movement. Her actions inspired countless others to stand up for their rights and challenge unjust systems. In both of these cases, the information available to both these individuals would have only posted them to one thing, to maintain the status quo and to not question.

The philosopher Immanuel Kant argued that the foundation of moral reasoning is the idea of autonomy, or the ability to reason for oneself and determine one's own moral principles. This requires individuals to use their own judgment rather than relying on external authority figures or societal norms. Autonomy in our actions, autonomy in our beliefs, and autonomy in our thoughts is what sets us free.

By developing our own reasoning and judgment, we can make more informed decisions, challenge unjust systems, and ultimately lead more fulfilling lives.

❑

15

Letting Go Gives Us Freedom

To let go, is to set oneself free.

Letting go gives us freedom, and freedom is the only condition for happiness. If, in our heart, we still cling to anything—anger, anxiety, or possessions—we cannot be free.

—Thich nhat hang

The famous American author and poet Maya Angelou once said, “I've learned that people will forget what you said, people will forget what you did, but people will never forget how you made them feel.” This sentiment speaks to the idea of letting go of our attachment to material possessions and focusing on the intangible things that truly matter in life, such as our relationships with others. Letting go is not just about detachment from material things but also about valuing things that truly matter.

These immortal words of the famous Vietnamese Zen Master Thich Nhat Hanh teach us that attaching ourselves to anything which is even the slightest negative would mean we are living in the past, that we feel we own things when nothing is truly ours. We feel that we are owed something when in fact no one or nothing owes us anything. Letting go is a concept that has been discussed in ancient wisdom, such as Buddhism and Taoism, and is still relevant in modern times. It is the idea of relinquishing attachment to things that hold us back from happiness and freedom.

In Buddhism, the concept of 'attachment' is seen as the root cause of suffering. The Buddha taught that attachment to things that are impermanent, such as material possessions, relationships, and even our own physical bodies, leads to a never-ending cycle of craving and dissatisfaction. By letting go of these attachments, we can free ourselves from suffering and find inner peace.

From a psychological perspective, letting go of negative emotions like anger and anxiety can have a profound impact on our mental health. Studies have shown that holding on to negative emotions can lead to chronic stress, which has a detrimental effect on both our physical and mental well-being. By learning to let go of these emotions, we can reduce stress and increase our overall sense of well-being.

The Stoics believed that we should not be attached to things that are beyond our control, such as the actions of other people or the changing circumstances of life. By accepting that these things are outside of our control and learning to let go of our attachment to them, we can find peace and contentment in the present moment.

From a practical perspective, letting go of material possessions can also be liberating. We live in a world that often equates happiness and success with the accumulation of material goods. However, studies have shown that the more possessions we have, the less happy we are. The illusion of choice is also a well-established and studied fact. In the consumer-driven culture where more is good and more choices are always better, it has been found that after a point, choices, in fact, make us less efficient and only add to our indecision. By letting go of our attachment to material possessions, we can free ourselves from the burden of constantly acquiring and maintaining these objects and focus on the things that truly bring us joy and fulfillment.

Letting go is a powerful concept that can bring us freedom, happiness and inner peace. It is the act of relinquishing attachment to things that hold us back from living a fulfilling life. Whether it is letting go of negative emotions, material possessions, or our attachment to things outside of our control, the act of letting go can have a profound impact on our well-being. As Thich Nhat Hanh said, "Letting go gives us freedom, and freedom is the only condition for happiness. Let go of what has passed. Let go of what may come. Let go of what is happening now. Don't try to figure anything out. Don't try to make anything happen. Relax, right now, and rest."

❑

16

A Jug Fills Drop by Drop

Biggest of the vessels are filled one drop at a time.

A jug fills drop by drop.

—The Buddha

This quote is attributed to the Buddha and has been used to convey the message of persistence and consistency in achieving our goals. It is a reminder that even small actions can accumulate to create significant progress over time. In this chapter, we will delve deeper into the meaning of this quote and explore how it applies to our lives. It reminds us of the fact that nothing happens overnight, no big goal is achieved in a day and to do or accomplish great feats, one needs to focus on being consistent.

In many areas of our lives, we tend to focus on the end result. We set goals and targets and tend to forget the process which is supposed to be undertaken well in order to get there. What happens after that is that the end goal, the main mission seems overwhelming, and we often get discouraged when we don't see immediate progress. However, we must always remind ourselves that progress doesn't happen all at once; it happens gradually, little by little. It's the small steps that we take consistently that add up to the bigger picture. Be it finance or human efforts, compounding is a powerful phenomenon.

The *Tao Te Ching* says: "A journey of a thousand miles begins with a single step." The message is clear: every accomplishment starts with one small step. We must walk before we run and we must stand before we walk; we have to learn to respect the process.

It is no hidden service, that small actions add up over time. In a study published in the *European Journal of Social Psychology*, researchers found that it takes an average of 66 days to form a new habit. The key to forming a habit is consistency and repetition, which means that small actions performed daily can have a significant impact over time. Many times we tend to pick up tasks that are challenging as it is but then we are impatient to give them enough time or give ourselves enough time. We want instant results.

The value of patience and understanding this phenomenon affects our mental well-being as well. Not only do we put ourselves under undue pressure when we act impatiently and seek immediate and short-term gratification, but we also hurt our chances of succeeding at something anytime in the future as fair caused due to impatience don't register like that, it registers us as a failure.

In philosophy, the concept of gradual progress is talked about quite often. Aristotle believed that excellence is not an act, but a habit. In other words, the small actions we take consistently are what lead to excellence in the long run. Confucius believed that 'it does not matter how slowly you go as long as you do not stop'. The importance and the power of compounding are not felt for the first few months, but one fine day you start noticing substantial changes; to reach that one day, you need to keep working consistently. Olympic gold medalist Michael Phelps trained every day for years, constantly pushing himself to improve his performance. His success was not achieved overnight but was the result of consistent effort.

The small actions we take every day may seem insignificant, but they add up over time and lead to significant progress. It's a reminder that we don't have to achieve everything all at once; we just need to keep moving forward, one step at a time. Whether it's physical or mental health, career success, or personal growth, we can achieve anything we set our minds to if we stay committed and take consistent action.

Just like physical health, mental health requires consistent small actions to maintain. Engaging in daily practices such as meditation, journaling, or exercise may not seem like much, but over time, they can lead to significant improvements in our mental and emotional health.

❑

17
Knowing You Know Nothing

Knowledge is a lifelong pursuit.

The only true wisdom is in knowing you know nothing.

— Socrates

Socrates, the ancient Greek philosopher, suggested that true wisdom is not just about acquiring knowledge but about recognizing one's limitations and acknowledging the vastness of the unknown. Socrates' statement reflects a central concept in philosophy, which is the idea of epistemological humility. Epistemology is the branch of philosophy that deals with knowledge and belief. Epistemological humility refers to the recognition that one's knowledge is limited, and that there is much that one does not know. This concept is echoed in other philosophical traditions, such as Taoism and Buddhism, where the emphasis is on acknowledging the limits of human understanding.

The idea of acknowledging what we don't know can be beneficial in more ways than one. In a study published in the *Journal of Personality and Social Psychology*, researchers found that individuals who scored high on a test of intellectual humility tended to be more open to new ideas and perspectives, more receptive to feedback, and less likely to hold onto rigid beliefs. These qualities are associated with better psychological well-being and more positive social interactions.

Acknowledging one's limitations can also lead to a growth mindset. Psychologist Carol Dweck has conducted extensive research on the concept of a growth mindset versus a fixed mindset. People with a fixed mindset believe that their abilities and traits are innate and cannot be changed, while those with a growth mindset believe that they can develop and improve over time. Embracing a growth mindset means acknowledging that there is always room for improvement and that even if you don't know something now, you can always learn later.

Albert Einstein once said, "The more I learn, the more I realize how much I don't know." A mind like Einstein's that comes once in a generation stating this is enough for us to be humble and accepting of our limitations and gaps.

Isaac Newton famously stated, "I do not know what I may appear to the world, but to myself, I seem to have been only like a boy playing on the seashore and diverting myself in now and then finding a smoother pebble or a prettier shell than ordinary, whilst the great ocean of truth lay all undiscovered before me." When the greatest minds ever to have walked on our planet agree on one thing, we ought to pay attention. In this case, that one thing is how little we can ever know.

High-achieving athletes who acknowledge their weaknesses and work to improve them often see the greatest growth and success. Michael Jordan, widely regarded as one of the greatest basketball players of all time, once said, "I've missed more than nine thousand shots in my career. I've lost almost three hundred games. Twenty-six times, I've been trusted to take the game-winning shot and missed. I've failed over and over and over again in my life. And that is why I succeed." Jordan's willingness to acknowledge his failures and work to improve allowed him to become one of the greatest athletes of all time.

'The only true wisdom is in knowing you know nothing' highlights the importance of epistemological humility and recognizing the limits of our knowledge. Embracing this mindset can lead to greater openness, receptivity to feedback, and growth. As demonstrated by ancient wisdom, scientific research, philosophy, and examples from the lives of famous people and athletes, acknowledging our limitations can be a powerful tool in achieving success and happiness.

❑

18

Happiness Never Decreases by being Shared

Our happiness is not truly just ours, share it.

Thousands of candles can be lit from a single candle,
and the life of the candle will not be shortened.
Happiness never decreases by being shared.

— The Buddha

This quote is a profound statement that highlights the importance of generosity, kindness and compassion. It speaks of the idea that by sharing our joy and happiness with others, we can increase our own sense of fulfillment and contentment. It also speaks about how wrong we are to consider our happiness ours alone, thinking that it's just because of our efforts and we have earned it for ourselves.

Ancient wisdom and philosophy have long recognized the power of generosity and its ability to bring joy to both the giver and the receiver. In Hinduism, the concept of '*dana*' or giving is one of the five *yamas,* or ethical principles, that one must follow in order to live a fulfilling life. The Buddhist concept of *dana* is also based on the idea that giving can lead to a sense of happiness and well-being.

The Greek philosopher Aristotle also believed that generosity was an important virtue, stating, "The generous person is the one who gives to the right people, the right amounts, and at the right times."

The idea of giving is not a selfish act, it is not done hoping that something good would happen to us, it is done because one understands that at times it is one's good fortune to find oneself in the capacity to do something or give. The act of giving is done as a matter of duty, as Kant would've said.

Modern scientific research has also shown the positive effects of generosity on our overall well-being. A study published in the journal, *Social Science & Medicine* found that people who regularly give to others report higher levels of happiness and lower levels of depression and anxiety. Additionally, a study conducted by the University of Zurich found that when people give money to others, the pleasure centres of their brains are activated, leading to increased feelings of happiness. Altruism has come to be recognised as a dopamine and serotonin booster globally, but the truth of the act of giving must be done even when one feels great as it is.

Psychology also recognizes the power of generosity and the positive impact it can have on our mental health. The act of giving can lead to a sense of purpose and fulfillment, which can help combat feelings of loneliness, depression and anxiety. Moreover, research has shown that generosity can foster stronger relationships with others, leading to a greater sense of social support and community.

Mother Teresa, a Catholic nun and missionary, dedicated her life to helping others and spreading joy to those in need. She once said, "I alone cannot change the world, but I can cast a stone across the waters to create many ripples." This exemplifies the idea that by sharing our love and compassion with others, we can create a positive impact that extends far beyond ourselves.

Athletes often use their platform and success to give back to their communities and support charitable causes. Michael Jordan, one of the greatest basketball players of all time, is known for his philanthropic efforts, including the creation of the Jordan Fundamentals programme, which provides education and sports programmes to underprivileged children.

'Thousands of candles can be lit from a single candle, and the life of the candle will not be shortened. Happiness never decreases by being shared' emphasises the importance of generosity and sharing happiness with others and the power of generosity in promoting well-being and creating positive change in the world. By embracing generosity and kindness, we can cultivate greater happiness and fulfillment in our own lives and the lives of those around us.

❑

19

Evil Friend Will Wound Your Mind

A small circle, a meaningful circle is better than a circus.

An insincere and evil friend is more to be feared than a wild beast; a wild beast may wound your body, but an evil friend will wound your mind.

— The Buddha

The people we surround ourselves with have a profound impact on our lives, and this is something that has been recognized throughout history.

The great Greek philosopher Aristotle spoke about the importance of friendships, and how they can bring happiness and meaning to our lives. Similarly, in the Eastern tradition of Buddhism, it is believed that our relationships with others are essential for our personal growth and development. The concept of 'Sangha' or community, emphasizes the importance of being part of a supportive and uplifting group. The importance that has been given to the company we keep and to the nature and quality of the company can't be understated. More often than not, we become what we have around us. It does mean that someone born unfortunate and having no choice would remain that way; what it means is that we need to work to change our fortune and seek company that can help us do that. We do not need to seek people to use them; instead, we must seek company with people who can teach us and from whom we get to learn, and as a result grow as human beings.

A lot of research and several studies have also shown the importance of friendships in our lives. Studies have found that having strong social connections can increase our happiness and well-being, reduce stress, and even improve our physical health. On the other hand, negative or toxic relationships can have detrimental effects on our mental health and well-being.

The psychology of friendships is also a complex and fascinating topic. It is said that we are the average of the five people we spend the most time with, and this is backed up by research. We are influenced by the beliefs, values and behaviours of those around us, whether we are aware of it or not. This is why it is so important to surround ourselves with positive and supportive individuals who share our values and aspirations. But this also has a catch. We tend to mingle with people who reinforce our biases, our weaknesses, our partial judgements, and share our worldview and thus we seldom get a chance to listen to and hear others' perspectives on things. There must be a fine balance. We should avoid negative people but just because someone disagrees with us, they should not be treated or thought of as negative.

This quote highlights the potential harm that negative relationships can have on our mental and emotional well-being. An insincere friend is someone who is not genuine or authentic in their interactions with us. They may pretend to be supportive or caring, but their true intentions are selfish or malicious. An evil friend, on the other hand, actively seeks to harm us and undermine our well-being. A lot of people have the capacity to fake for a long time. till the end, they can act, they can pretend for ages, It is very important that we set high standards about who we let in our lives and with whom we share secrets and our lives and our insecurities and our vulnerabilities.

In Shakespeare's play *Julius Caesar*, the character Brutus is convinced by his friend Cassius to betray Caesar and join the conspiracy to assassinate him. Despite his initial reservations, Brutus is swayed by Cassius' arguments and ultimately becomes consumed by guilt and regret. There are numerous examples in history when the downfall comes from within and not outside and that is often because of the people close to us.

We can see the impact of negative friendships on the rise of cyberbullying and online harassment. Social media platforms can be a breeding ground for toxic relationships, as individuals hide behind anonymity and lash out at others with little regard for the consequences. The mental health consequences of cyberbullying can be severe, leading to depression, anxiety and even suicide in extreme cases.

We must understand and appreciate the importance of choosing our friends wisely. Positive and supportive relationships can bring us joy and happiness, while negative or toxic relationships can have detrimental effects on our mental and emotional well-being. It is important to surround ourselves with individuals who share our values and aspirations, and who uplift and support us on our journey through life.

❑

20

Smile is the Beginning of Love

A smile can make your day.

Let us always meet each other with a smile, for the smile is the beginning of Love.

— Mother Teresa

This is a quote from Mother Teresa, inspired by ancient Buddhist philosophy, stressing the power of positivity, kindness and empathy. This quote is a powerful reminder of the importance of kindness and the impact it can have on our lives and the lives of those around us.

In today's fast-paced and stressful world, it can be easy to get caught up in our worries and concerns, forgetting the importance of connecting with others. Smiling is a simple but effective way to begin to break down the barriers that can exist between us and others. It is a universal language that transcends cultural and language barriers and can help us to create more positive relationships with those around us. It is not just about the literal act of smiling but being kind to strangers, without expecting anything in return, helping someone in need without hoping for recognition; it is much more than just a smile. But, even a smile is a great place to start. You never know what kind of a day someone is having and your smile might make it a bit better for them.

Ancient wisdom has long recognized the power of random acts of kindness. In the *Tao Te Ching*, Lao Tzu wrote, "Kindness in words creates confidence. Kindness in thinking creates profoundness. Kindness in giving creates love." The act of smiling is also a form of kindness, and as Lao Tzu suggests, it can create confidence, profoundness and love, not just for the one whom the smile is but for the one who smiles, it is an absolute win-win. Mahatma Gandhi, a leader in the Indian independence movement, once said, "We shall never know all the good that a simple smile can do."

Modern scientific research also supports the importance of a simple smile. Studies have shown that smiling can have a positive effect on our mental and physical well-being. Smiling releases endorphins, which are natural painkillers and mood elevators. It can also lower stress levels, reduce blood pressure, and boost our immune system. Additionally, smiling can help us to connect with others, making us more likeable and approachable. In fact, just activating the muscles involved in the act of smiling signals the brain that it is a happy time and it gets to work.

Psychology also recognizes the importance of a smile. Positive psychology, in particular, focuses on the role of positive emotions in our lives. A smile is a powerful positive emotion that can have a ripple effect, creating a more positive environment for ourselves and those around us. It can also help us to cultivate a more optimistic outlook on life.

Philosophers have long recognized and argued the importance of kindness and love. The ancient Greeks had several words for different types of love, including *philia* (friendship love) and *agape* (unconditional love). In his famous work, *The Symposium*, Plato discusses the nature of love and its ability to connect us with others. Friendship and love, kindness and empathy, all of it, starts with a simple smile.

Mother Teresa dedicated her life to serving the poor and sick, recognizing the importance of compassion and kindness. She helped people and worked for them and always did so with a smile.

Muhammad Ali considered one of the greatest boxers of all time, tough as they come, was known for his charismatic personality but also for his infectious smile. His positivity and charisma helped him to connect with fans and opponents alike, making him a beloved figure both inside and outside the ring.

Your smile is a powerful reminder of the importance of kindness, compassion and love in our lives. Whether we are facing difficult challenges or simply going about our day-to-day lives, a smile can be a powerful tool to help us connect with others, boost our mood, and create a more positive environment for ourselves and those around us.

❑

21

You Think You Have Time

Time is not one of the things, it's the only thing.

The trouble is, you think you have time.

— The Buddha

Time is a precious commodity, yet it is something that many of us take for granted. We often find ourselves saying, "I'll do it tomorrow" or "I'll have more time later," but the truth is, we never know how much time we have. We forget that time is finite, and we should not waste it on things that do not matter. We forget that time does not and won't wait for us or anyone. It goes on, the clock keeps on ticking.

Ancient works and wisdom have long warned us of the fleeting nature of time. In the *Tao Te Ching*, Lao Tzu wrote:

"Time is a created thing. To say 'I don't have time', is like saying, 'I don't want to'." When we say we have time or we will find time, what we essentially are saying is that we don't want to do it or that it is not important. 'We will find time' or 'We don't have time' are nothing but plain excuses. The great Greek philosopher Heraclitus once said, "Time is a game played beautifully by children." These words serve as a reminder that we have a choice in how we spend our time and that it is a precious resource that we should not waste. The cruel reality, the harsh truth about time is that we always feel that we control it or that we decide its fate, but nothing can be farther from the truth. We do not control time, time controls us. Time controls our very existence.

One of the ways in which we waste a lot of time is what is known as the 'planning fallacy', a cognitive bias where we tend to underestimate the time it takes to complete a task. This bias can lead us to believe we have more time than we actually do, which can result in procrastination and missed opportunities. As it is famously said, "The task at hand would grow to occupy all the time we have." Yet another aspect of how we are played psychologically comes from the concept of 'time perspective', which refers to the way we view time and how it influences our behaviour. People who have a future-oriented time perspective tend to be more proactive and goal-oriented, while those with a present-oriented perspective are more likely to focus on immediate pleasures and rewards.

Many studies have also shown the importance of time management and how we think and treat time as an entity in our lives. Studies have found that time perception can influence our emotions, behaviours, and decision-making.

Philosophers throughout history have also reflected on the concept of time. Seneca, the Stoic philosopher, wrote: "It is not that we have a short time to live, but that we waste a lot of it." This statement emphasizes the importance of making the most of our time, rather than squandering it on things that do not matter.

What it also means to say is that the limited time we have must not be spent on things that we don't really want to do, but rather on things that we love.

Steve Jobs, the late co-founder of Apple, once famously said, "Your time is limited, don't waste it living someone else's life." This shows the importance of being true to ourselves and pursuing our own passions, rather than living up to someone else's expectations. A lot of our time is wasted because we worry too much about what people would think and how they will react and thus a lot of our time goes into pleasing other people, people who don't really matter.

We have limited time and we have to make the most of it and we have to put every second to good use. Michael Jordan, the legendary basketball player, once said, "I always felt that my greatest asset was not my physical ability, it was my mental ability to make the most of my time and my talent."

Ancient works, scientific research, psychology, philosophy, and examples from the lives of famous people throughout history and sports all emphasize the importance of time and making the most of it. By being mindful of how we spend our time, we can live more fulfilling lives and achieve our goals.

❑

22

No One Saves Us But Ourselves

You may meet many fellow passengers, but you are always alone.

No one saves us but ourselves. No one can and no one may.
We ourselves must walk the path.

— The Buddha

There is a concept in Buddhism, known as 'self-liberation' or 'self-realization'. The Buddha taught that in life, no external force or deity can save us from the suffering we experience. Instead, we must take responsibility for our happiness and liberation. We should cultivate mindfulness and awareness of our thoughts, emotions and behaviours and develop positive qualities such as compassion, wisdom and generosity. We cannot and must not wait for a saviour to come and rescue us; no one is coming. This is a powerful reminder of the importance of taking responsibility for our lives and being the masters of our destinies.

This idea is also present in modern psychology, in the concept of self-efficacy, which refers to our belief in our ability to control our own lives and achieve our goals. Research has shown that individuals with high levels of self-efficacy are more likely to be successful in achieving their goals, both in their personal and professional lives.

The idea of taking responsibility for our own lives is also central to many philosophical traditions. In the writings of the Stoics, for example, individuals are encouraged to focus on what they can control in life rather than worrying about external factors beyond their control. This can help individuals to develop a sense of inner strength and resilience, even in the face of difficult circumstances.

Nelson Mandela spent 27 years in prison for his activism against apartheid in South Africa. Despite the difficult circumstances, Mandela never lost his sense of inner strength and resilience. He once said, "I am the master of my fate, I am the captain of my soul," emphasizing the importance of taking responsibility for one's own life. These famous lines come from the poem 'Invictus' by William Ernest Henley. These lines have been used as a source of inspiration and motivation for countless people for over a century. The sentiment expressed in these lines is that we have the power to control our own destiny and that we are responsible for the course of our lives.

The concept of being in control of our own lives is not a new one. Philosophers and thinkers throughout history have emphasised the importance of taking personal responsibility for our actions and decisions. In ancient Greece, the philosopher Aristotle argued that we are responsible for our own happiness and well-being. In the 19th century, Friedrich Nietzsche wrote extensively about the importance of personal responsibility and the will to power.

Scientific research also supports the idea that taking control of our lives can have a positive impact on our mental and physical health. Studies have found that people who feel in control of their lives tend to be less stressed and experience less anxiety and depression. They also tend to have better physical health and longevity.

Psychologists have identified a concept known as 'locus of control' that refers to the extent to which individuals believe they have control over the events that affect their lives. People with an internal locus of control believe that their actions and decisions can impact their lives, while those with an external locus of control believe that their lives are controlled by external forces such as fate or luck.

Another example is Stephen Hawking, who despite being diagnosed with ALS at a young age, went on to become one of the greatest minds of our time. He said, "My expectations were reduced to zero when I was 21. Everything since then has been a bonus." He didn't let his disability define him or limit his potential.

In sports too, this message is often embodied in the idea of 'mental toughness'. Athletes who are able to maintain a positive attitude and focus on their goals, even in the face of adversity, are often the most successful. To be successful requires a strong sense of self-belief and the ability to overcome negative self-talk and self-doubt. Michael Jordan, widely regarded as one of the greatest basketball players of all time, was cut from his high school basketball team. Rather than giving up, he used the experience as motivation to work harder and become a better player.

'We ourselves must walk the path' is a powerful reminder of the importance of taking responsibility for our own lives. This message can be found in many ancient works, including Buddhism and Stoicism, and is also relevant in modern psychology and self-help. By cultivating mindfulness, self-efficacy, and a sense of inner strength and resilience, we can take control of our own lives and achieve our goals, both personal and professional.

❑

23

Mind is Like a Parachute

An open mind is the laboratory where all experiments are done.

The mind is like a parachute; it only works when it is open.
— Frank Zappa

This quote, often attributed to Frank Zappa, inspired by ancient Buddhist thought, is a powerful reminder of the importance of an open and curious mindset. In this context, an open mind refers to a willingness to explore new ideas, perspectives and experiences without preconceived notions or biases.

Ancient wisdom from various cultures, including Buddhism and Taoism, has long recognized the importance of an open mind. The *Tao Te Ching*, for instance, speaks of the importance of emptying the mind and embracing the present moment. In any approach, you should shed preconceived notions and have no bias. This way, you stand a chance to learn from every experience and a chance to appreciate every experience.

In Buddhism, the concept of the Beginner's Mind encourages us to approach every situation with a curious and non-judgmental attitude, as if we were experiencing it for the first time. It is important to be a child when you are presented with something new, ask as many questions as you wish, and explore.

Modern scientific research also supports the idea that an open mind is essential for growth and development. Studies have shown that people with open-minded attitudes are more likely to be creative, adaptable and successful in their personal and professional lives. In contrast, those with closed or rigid mindsets are more likely to experience anxiety, stress and even depression. It is a very straightforward thing. In fact, the more you are willing to seek and open to learning, the higher your chances to grow.

Psychology and philosophy have long studied the relationship between the mind and behaviour. One popular concept is the 'fixed mindset' versus the 'growth mindset'. People with fixed mindset believe that their abilities are set in stone and are less likely to take risks or try new things. In contrast, those with a growth mindset believe that their abilities can be developed and improved over time through hard work and dedication. The latter group is more likely to be open-minded, as they are constantly seeking out new challenges and experiences to learn and grow from. People with a fixed mindset are risk averse, they are less likely to try on new things, less likely to learn new skills, and as a result less likely to grow.

Albert Einstein once said, "I have no special talent, I am only passionately curious." His curiosity and willingness to explore new ideas and theories led him to develop groundbreaking scientific concepts that changed the world.

Similarly, Steve Jobs, the founder of Apple, was known for his ability to think outside the box and come up with innovative solutions to complex problems. His openness to new ideas and willingness to take risks led him to create one of the most successful companies in history.

Athletes who are open to trying new training techniques, exploring different strategies, and listening to feedback from coaches and teammates are more likely to improve and reach their goals. In contrast, those who are resistant to change or new ideas may become stuck in a rut and struggle to achieve their full potential.

Richard Feynman, one of the most widely celebrated geniuses was a curious should before he was anything, he preferred to be a student all his life and that's what made him the best teacher.

'The mind is like a parachute; it only works when it is open' emphasizes the importance of an open and curious mindset. By cultivating a willingness to explore new ideas, perspectives and experiences, we can expand our horizons, develop new skills and abilities, and achieve our full potential.

❑

24
Relationship Between Equals

Compassion is not charity.

Compassion is not a relationship between the healer and the wounded. It's a relationship between equals.

— Pema Chödrön

Compassion is an essential quality of human nature that drives us to connect with others and extend a helping hand to those in need. It's a universal language that transcends all cultural and social barriers and brings people together. Compassion is often seen as a trait that is inherent in healers or caregivers, but the truth is that it is something that can be practiced by anyone, regardless of their profession or status.

"Compassion has been hailed as a relationship between equals," says Pema Chödrön, a renowned Buddhist nun and author. According to Chödrön, the traditional concept of compassion as a hierarchical relationship between a caregiver and a patient is flawed. It creates a power dynamic in which the caregiver is seen as superior to the patient, leading to feelings of pity, shame or guilt. This dynamic can be damaging to both parties, as it creates an imbalance in the relationship and reinforces the notion that the patient is weak and helpless. It also presents compassion which is supposed to be an inherent human value and something which must be present in everyone as charity done by the strong towards the weak.

True compassion should be seen as a relationship between equals. It's about acknowledging the shared humanity between two individuals and recognizing that we are all vulnerable and in need of support at some point in our lives. When we approach others with a sense of equality and mutual respect, we create a space for connection and understanding that can lead to healing and growth.

Ancient wisdom traditions like Buddhism have long recognized the importance of compassion in human life In Buddhist teachings, compassion is one of the four 'immeasurables', along with loving-kindness, empathetic joy, and equanimity. It is seen as a powerful antidote to the suffering and struggles of life and is considered essential for achieving enlightenment.

The Dalai Lama, one of the most prominent spiritual leaders of our time, is a strong advocate for compassion and has dedicated his life to promoting its practice and cultivation.

Modern scientific research has also shown that compassion has numerous benefits for both mental and physical health. Studies have found that compassionate individuals tend to have lower levels of stress and anxiety, stronger immune systems, and more fulfilling relationships. Moreover, compassionate behaviour is contagious and can create a ripple effect of kindness and positivity in our communities. If someone is nice to you, you tend to remember it and try to be nice to others as you feel that there are people who care. When someone is rude to you, you feel that that is how people are in general.

The great Greek philosopher Aristotle believed that compassion was an essential component of virtuous behaviour and saw it as a key to living a meaningful and fulfilling life. Similarly, psychologist Carl Rogers emphasized the importance of empathy and unconditional positive regard in therapeutic relationships, which are based on the principles of compassion and equality.

Mahatma Gandhi, known for his nonviolent resistance to oppression, embodied compassion in his work to create a more just and peaceful world. Nelson Mandela, the former president of South Africa, also demonstrated immense compassion and forgiveness in his efforts to end apartheid and promote reconciliation.

Sportsmen have also shown the power of compassion in action. In the 1968 Olympics, Tommie Smith and John Carlos, two African American athletes, raised their fists in a Black Power salute during the medal ceremony to protest racial injustice. Their act of compassion and solidarity with the Black community sparked controversy but also inspired many to speak out against discrimination and fight for equality. The image has gone on to be immortalised in any and all fights against inequality and discrimination across the globe.

The quote 'Compassion is not a relationship between the healer and the wounded. It's a relationship between equals' emphasizes the importance of compassion as a fundamental aspect of human nature that transcends social and cultural barriers. It is a powerful force that can bring people together and promote healing and growth.

❑

25
Get Your Head Together First

Conquer yourself before you conquer the world.

In order to change the world, you have to get your head together first.

— Jimi Hendrix

The statement 'In order to change the world, you have to get your head together first' is a call of action to individuals to work on themselves before attempting to make a difference in the world. This quote emphasizes the importance of self-improvement and personal development as a precursor to making any meaningful change in the world.

Ancient religions such as Taoism and Buddhism teach the importance of self-awareness and self-cultivation in order to achieve inner peace and ultimately contribute to the greater good.

The Taoist principle of Wu Wei, or ‘action through inaction’, teaches the importance of quieting the mind and aligning oneself with the natural flow of the universe before taking any action.

Wu Wei translates to ‘non-action’ or ‘doing nothing’. It is often misunderstood as doing nothing at all, but in reality, it is more about ‘effortless action’ or ‘action without force’. It is a way of being in the world that emphasizes naturalness and spontaneity, rather than striving and struggle. This stage of effortless action can only be achieved when one is ready to work on their own self with nature.

Carl Jung’s concept of individuation emphasizes the process of becoming a fully realized and integrated individual, which includes developing self-awareness and working on oneself. This process of self-discovery and personal growth is also a necessary step in contributing to social change and making a positive impact in the world.

Buddhism emphasizes the practice of mindfulness and meditation as a means of cultivating inner wisdom and compassion. One way in which mindfulness and meditation cultivate inner wisdom and compassion is by helping individuals become more aware of their own thoughts, emotions and behaviors. Through these practices, individuals learn to observe their inner experiences with a non-judgmental and compassionate attitude, which can lead to greater self-awareness and self-understanding. This increased self-awareness can then translate into greater empathy and compassion for others, as individuals become more attuned to the experiences of others and more capable of understanding and empathizing with their struggles and challenges.

Moreover, mindfulness and meditation can help individuals cultivate a sense of inner peace and calm, even amid difficult and challenging circumstances. This inner peace and calm can then serve as a foundation for greater wisdom and compassion, as individuals become less reactive to external stimuli and more capable of responding with wisdom and compassion to the world around them.

Philosophers throughout history have also emphasized the importance of self-improvement for creating positive change in the world. The ancient Greek philosopher Socrates famously stated, "The unexamined life is not worth living," emphasizing the importance of self-reflection and introspection for personal growth and development. Similarly, the philosopher Aristotle believed that individuals should cultivate virtues such as wisdom, courage and compassion in order to contribute to the greater good of society.

Mahatma Gandhi, who led India to independence through non-violent resistance, famously said, "Be the change you want to see in the world." His life's work was grounded in his personal values and commitment to self-improvement, which enabled him to inspire and lead a movement for social justice.

Scientific research has also shown the benefits of self-improvement for achieving success and making a positive impact in the world. Studies have found that individuals with a growth mindset, who believe that their abilities and qualities can be improved through effort and learning, are more likely to achieve success in their pursuits. Developing a growth mindset involves working on oneself, including overcoming limiting beliefs and developing a positive attitude toward challenges.

In the world of sports, athletes also recognize the importance of personal development for achieving success and making a positive impact.

Athletes have long recognized the importance of personal development for achieving success and making a positive impact on the world around them. From basketball players like LeBron James and Kobe Bryant to tennis stars like Serena Williams and Roger Federer, athletes at the top of their game have often espoused the benefits of personal growth and development.

One key area of focus for athletes has been mental and emotional development. Through practices like mindfulness, meditation and visualization, athletes can cultivate the mental clarity and emotional resilience needed to perform at their best in high-pressure situations. Studies have shown that these practices can help athletes reduce stress, improve focus and concentration, and develop greater self-awareness and self-regulation skills.

But personal development is not just about improving one's own performance. Many athletes have also used their platforms to make a positive impact on the world around them. LeBron James, for example, has been an outspoken advocate for social justice issues, using his voice and resources to support causes like voting rights, education, and criminal justice reform. Soccer player Megan Rapinoe has similarly used her platform to advocate for gender equality and LGBTQ rights.

Athletes have also recognized the importance of physical development as part of personal growth. Through regular training and conditioning, athletes can improve their physical strength, endurance and agility, enabling them to perform at their best on the field or court. But beyond their own performance, many athletes have also used their physical prowess to make a difference in the world. Basketball player Kevin Durant, for example, has been involved in numerous philanthropic initiatives focused on improving the lives of children and families in underserved communities. The statement 'In order to change the world, you have to get your head together first' emphasizes the importance of self-improvement and personal development as a prerequisite for making a meaningful impact in the world.

❑

26

Greatest Victory is Victory Over Oneself

Caption

The greatest victory is victory over oneself.

— **Aristotle**

The concept of victory over oneself has been a recurring theme in many ancient and modern texts. It is the idea that true success and achievement are not just about defeating others, but rather about mastering one's thoughts, feelings and actions. This idea can be found in various philosophies, religions, and practices throughout history, such as Buddhism, Stoicism, and the philosophy of yoga.

In Buddhism, the concept of victory over oneself is central to the idea of enlightenment. The Buddha taught that the key to achieving inner peace and freedom from suffering is to overcome one's ignorance, attachment and aversion. This involves recognizing the impermanence and interconnectedness of all things and cultivating mindfulness, compassion and wisdom.

Similarly, in Stoicism, the goal is to achieve inner peace and happiness by mastering one's thoughts and emotions. The Stoics believed that true freedom and strength come from being able to control one's reactions to external events, rather than being controlled by them.

In yoga, the concept of victory over oneself is embodied in the practice of self-discipline and self-control. Through various physical and mental practices, such as asanas, pranayama and meditation, practitioners aim to purify and strengthen the mind and body, ultimately leading to spiritual liberation.

The idea of victory over oneself has also been embraced by many successful individuals throughout history. For example, Mahatma Gandhi, famously said, "The enemy is inside me. I am the enemy." He recognized that true change and progress could only come from overcoming his weaknesses and limitations. This sentiment has been expressed in various forms throughout history and across cultures. For example, the ancient Greek philosopher Plato wrote: "The first and greatest victory is to conquer yourself." Similarly, in the *Tao Te Ching*, the foundational text of Taoism, the emphasis is on cultivating inner harmony and balance in order to achieve external success and fulfillment. The concept of the 'shadow self' in Jungian psychology also speaks to the idea of acknowledging and integrating our negative traits and impulses in order to achieve greater wholeness and self-acceptance.

Similarly, Muhammad Ali, the world-renowned boxer and social activist, believed that true greatness came from overcoming oneself. He once said, "The fight is won or lost far away from witnesses—behind the lines, in the gym and out there on the road, long before I dance under those lights." Ali understood that victory in the ring was not just about physical strength, but also about mental discipline and self-mastery.

Modern psychological research also supports the idea that victory over oneself is key to achieving success and happiness. Studies have shown that self-control and self-discipline are strong predictors of academic and career success, as well as overall well-being. Additionally, mindfulness practices such as meditation have been shown to increase emotional regulation, reduce stress and anxiety, and improve cognitive functioning.

In order to apply this principle to our own lives, it is important to first cultivate a sense of self-awareness and introspection. This can be achieved through practices such as mindfulness meditation, journaling or therapy. By becoming more aware of our thoughts and behaviors, we can begin to identify patterns and tendencies that may be holding us back.

Once we have identified areas in which we need to improve, it is important to take action and hold ourselves accountable. This may involve setting goals, seeking support from others, or seeking professional help. By taking responsibility for our own growth and development, we can begin to break free from negative patterns and achieve greater success and fulfillment in all areas of our lives.

The concept of victory over oneself is a powerful and timeless idea that has been embraced by various cultures and individuals throughout history. By mastering our thoughts, feelings and actions, we can achieve true success, happiness and inner peace. Whether through religious or philosophical practices, personal development, or psychological techniques, the journey of self-mastery is a rewarding and fulfilling one that can lead to a lifetime of growth and fulfillment.

❑

27
Better to Travel Well than to Arrive

The journey well made matters more.

It is better to travel well than to arrive.

— The Buddha

The quote 'It is better to travel well than to arrive' may seem puzzling at first glance. After all, isn't the destination, the whole point of travelling? However, this quote by Buddha encapsulates a deeper meaning beyond the physical act of traveling. It's about the journey itself and how we approach it; both the internal journey of personal growth and the external journey of encountering various difficulties on the way and taking them in stride, learning all along.

One way to look at this quote is that the process of growth and self-discovery is more important than the end goal. It's not just about achieving a particular outcome or arriving at a destination, but rather, it's about the process of getting there. The journey provides opportunities for learning, growth and personal transformation. In fact, some argue that the journey is the destination.

There are many ancient works and wisdom that highlight the importance of the journey. The *Tao Te Ching,* an ancient Chinese text, emphasizes the importance of the journey and the process of self-discovery. It states: "The journey of a thousand miles begins with one step." This quote highlights that the journey is a gradual process that starts with a single step. It also means that each and every step is equally important no matter how long the journey is. It also means that in order to complete a long journey, it is important to ensure that one appreciates the value of each and every stop, milestone, detour, roadblock and everything else one encounters.

The famous Greek philosopher Aristotle believed that the journey towards our goals is more important than the goals themselves. He believed that the journey of learning and growing is what leads to true fulfillment and happiness.

From a psychological perspective, the idea of enjoying the journey rather than focusing solely on the outcome is also supported by research. A study by psychologists Ryan and Deci found that people who focus on the process of their goals and enjoy the journey are more likely to achieve long-term success and happiness.

In addition, the process of striving for a goal is often accompanied by stress and pressure. This can lead to burnout, anxiety and decreased motivation. However, by focusing on the journey, we can reduce the negative impact of stress and pressure by enjoying the process and finding meaning in the small steps we take along the way. We need to focus on the task at hand without worrying too much about the outcome as it can create undue pressure and harm us in our endeavours.

The importance of enjoying the journey can be seen in the lives of famous people throughout history. Thomas Edison, for example, failed over a thousand times before successfully inventing the light bulb. Despite facing numerous setbacks, he continued to enjoy the journey of discovery and experimentation. Similarly, basketball player Michael Jordan is known for his intense work ethic and focus on the process of improvement. In fact, athletes often train for years to achieve their goals, but it's the daily practice and small improvements that lead to success. In fact, athletes who enjoy the process of training and competing are more likely to achieve long-term success and fulfillment.

The quote 'It is better to travel well than to arrive' highlights the importance of enjoying the journey rather than focusing solely on the outcome. This concept is supported by ancient wisdom, psychological research, and the lives of famous people throughout history. By focusing on the journey, we can find fulfillment in the process of growth and personal transformation.

❑

28

Purpose in this Life is to Help Others

Give what you can, without expecting a return.

Our prime purpose in this life is to help others. And if you can't help them, at least don't hurt them.

— The Dalai Lama

The idea of helping others has been a central tenet of many philosophical and spiritual traditions for centuries. From the ancient Greek philosophers to religious figures like Jesus and Buddha, the message has been consistent: the highest purpose of our lives is to serve others. And while the concept may seem simple enough, in practice it can be more difficult to live out.

In today's fast-paced and competitive world, it's easy to become focused solely on our own success and achievement. We can easily forget the impact our actions have on those around us, and the responsibility we have to use our talents and resources for the greater good. However, the truth is that helping others is not only a moral imperative, but it also has significant benefits for our own well-being.

Research in positive psychology has shown that individuals who engage in acts of kindness and service to others experience greater levels of happiness, life satisfaction, and overall well-being. These acts can be as simple as holding the door open for someone or volunteering for a local charity. They don't have to be grand gestures to have a significant impact on both the recipient and the giver.

The idea of not hurting others is equally important. It's important to remember that our actions have consequences, and we have a responsibility to be mindful of how our choices impact those around us. Whether it's being mindful of our words and how they can hurt others or refraining from engaging in harmful behaviors, choosing to not hurt others is an essential part of being a compassionate and responsible member of society.

Mother Teresa, for example, spent her life serving the poor and sick in India, earning her a Nobel Peace Prize and sainthood in the Catholic church. Mahatma Gandhi dedicated himself to nonviolent resistance in India's struggle for independence from British rule. Martin Luther King Jr fought for civil rights and equality for African-Americans in the United States, ultimately sacrificing his life for the cause.

But helping others doesn't always have to involve grand gestures or changing the world on a large scale. We can all make a difference in our own way, whether it's through small acts of kindness, volunteering in our local communities, or simply being a good listener to a friend in need. Helping others is something that can be done by anyone and it does not require us to have access to a large amount of money or any other resource; all we need is intent and willingness to help. Helping others in need, and helping the less fortunate is always possible, all we need to do is to look around with intent and we would find people in dire need of our help and assistance.

In order to cultivate a mindset of helping others and avoiding harm, it's important to practice empathy and compassion. This involves putting ourselves in the shoes of others and considering their perspectives and experiences. When we are able to empathize with others, we are more likely to act in a way that is beneficial and supportive.

In addition to empathy and compassion, mindfulness can also be a powerful tool for developing a mindset of helping others. By being fully present in the moment and aware of our thoughts and actions, we are better able to make intentional choices that prioritize the needs of others.

Ultimately, the greatest purpose of our lives is not to accumulate wealth, power or fame, but to serve others and make a positive impact on the world. Whether through small acts of kindness or large-scale movements for social justice, each of us has the ability to contribute to a better world. And in doing so, we will find greater fulfillment and purpose in our own lives.

❑

29
Tilt Your Head Back and Laugh at the Sky

There is no beauty compared to nature.

When you realize how perfect everything is, you will tilt your head back and laugh at the sky.

— The Buddha

This quote, attributed to Buddha, is a reminder that even in the midst of chaos and uncertainty, there is a deep sense of perfection that exists in the world. It reminds us that nature always balances things out and that nature always takes care of everything. In the long term, the natural plan is far ahead of our ability to comprehend. But it does not mean that we are free to do as we please and there won't be any bad consequences. In fact, it means that nature's way is to balance the deeds, it is one of the karmic laws in play.

From ancient teachings to modern scientific research, the concept of mindfulness and present-moment awareness is one of the most powerful tools we can use to cultivate a sense of peace, gratitude and joy in our lives. By focusing on the present moment, we can let go of worry about the future or regret about the past and fully embrace the beauty and perfection of what is happening right now.

One ancient practice that has been shown to be particularly effective in cultivating mindfulness is meditation. By dedicating time each day to sit quietly and observe our thoughts without judgement, we can become more aware of our patterns of thinking and learn to let go of negative thoughts and emotions.

In addition to meditation, there are many other practices that can help us cultivate mindfulness, such as yoga, journaling, or spending time in nature. The key is to find what works for us and to make these practices a regular part of our routine.

This quote also has another perspective, which is, that nature is beyond our understanding. Its beauties and mysteries are beyond our comprehension. That we may complain and moan as much as we wish, but the beauty of nature and the simple yet detailed wonders it possesses are staring at us all the time, looking at us and smiling. It also stresses that we should be grateful for what we have and stop complaining all the time, be happy with the life we have, and be satisfied with what we have.

Beyond mindfulness, there are also many other ways we can cultivate a sense of gratitude and joy in our lives. One powerful practice is the expression of gratitude. By focusing on the things we are grateful for, we can shift our attention away from negative thoughts and emotions and cultivate a deep sense of appreciation for all that we have.

Research has shown that expressing gratitude can have a number of powerful benefits, including increased happiness, improved relationships, and better physical health. So whether it's writing in a gratitude journal or simply taking a moment each day to reflect on the things we are thankful for, expressing gratitude can be a powerful tool for cultivating joy and contentment.

Ultimately, the quote 'When you realize how perfect everything is, you will tilt your head back and laugh at the sky' reminds us that even in the midst of difficult times, there is always a deeper sense of perfection that exists in the world. By cultivating mindfulness, gratitude and joy in our lives, we can tap into this deeper sense of perfection and find peace and contentment even in the face of adversity.

The Dalai Lama, who has spent his life spreading a message of peace and compassion, and Mother Teresa, who dedicated her life to serving others and helping the less fortunate.

The quote 'When you realize how perfect everything is, you will tilt your head back and laugh at the sky' is a reminder of the power of mindfulness, gratitude, and joy in our lives. By cultivating these qualities, we can find peace and contentment even in the midst of difficulty, and ultimately live more fulfilling and meaningful lives.

❑

30

Be Kind Whenever Possible

Kindness is humanity's only hope.

Be kind whenever possible. It is always possible.

— The Dalai Lama

The phrase is often attributed to the 14th Dalai Lama, Tenzin Gyatso, inspired by the life of Lord Buddha. It encapsulates the fundamental principle of kindness that many spiritual and philosophical traditions emphasize. Kindness is an essential aspect of our human nature and has been recognized as a significant virtue throughout history.

From the teachings of the Buddha to the writings of Aristotle, philosophers and spiritual leaders have emphasized the importance of kindness in our daily lives. The ancient Greek philosopher, Aristotle, said, "Kindness is a virtue whose excess is rarely shown." Kindness is not just about being nice to others; it is about having compassion and empathy for others, treating them with respect and understanding, and acting in a way that uplifts and inspires others.

Scientific research has also shown that kindness can have a positive impact on our mental and physical health. Studies have found that practicing kindness can reduce stress, lower blood pressure, and improve our overall well-being. Acts of kindness have been shown to increase levels of dopamine, a neurotransmitter associated with feelings of pleasure and reward, and can also release oxytocin, a hormone that promotes social bonding and reduces stress.

Moreover, kindness has been shown to have a contagious effect, spreading from person to person and creating a positive ripple effect in our communities. Studies have found that acts of kindness can create a 'pay it forward' effect, inspiring others to engage in acts of kindness as well.

Mother Teresa was a Catholic nun who dedicated her life to serving the poor and marginalized in India. She founded the Missionaries of Charity, a religious congregation that provides care for people in need, including those with HIV/AIDS, leprosy and tuberculosis. Mother Teresa believed that kindness was a key component of serving others, and she lived her life as an example of selflessness and compassion.

Athletes have also recognized the importance of kindness, both on and off the field. Basketball player, Kevin Durant, once said, "Kindness is a mark of faith, and whoever has not kindness has not faith." Tennis player, Novak Djokovic, has emphasized the importance of kindness in his life, saying, "Kindness is the essence of all successful relationships, whether they are personal or professional."

Fred Rogers, also known as Mister Rogers, was a beloved children's television host known for his gentle demeanor and messages of kindness and acceptance. He believed that every person was deserving of love and respect, and he worked tirelessly to create a world where children felt valued and heard.

Small acts of kindness can have a big impact on someone's life. It can brighten their day, make them feel valued and appreciated, and even change the course of their life. When we show kindness to others, it can inspire them to pay it forward and show kindness to others as well. This can create a positive ripple effect that can spread throughout our communities and even the world. Being kind can improve our relationships with others. When we show kindness, empathy and compassion, we can build trust, respect and understanding. This can lead to deeper and more meaningful connections with others. Kindness can contribute to a more positive and compassionate world. When we show kindness to others, we are creating a more harmonious and inclusive community. This can lead to a more peaceful and equitable world for everyone.

'Be kind whenever possible. It is always possible' is a powerful reminder of the importance of kindness in our lives. Kindness is not only a virtue, but it also has a positive impact on our mental and physical health, creates a ripple effect in our communities, and is a central part of many individuals' lives throughout history. As we navigate through life, we should strive to be kind to others and ourselves, recognizing that even small acts of kindness can make a significant difference in the world.

❑

31
One-pointed Concentration

Focus to fight the evil of distraction.

Whatever you do, do it with one-pointed concentration

The quote emphasizes the importance of focus and concentration in achieving our goals. It suggests that we should give our undivided attention to the task at hand, rather than allowing our thoughts to wander or become distracted by external factors. Multitasking is not for everyone. In fact, almost everyone fails miserably at it. Our brain functions best when it enters the state of flow as described by Mihaly Csikszentmihalyi in his path-breaking work.

Ancient wisdom traditions have long recognized the importance of concentration and focus. In Hinduism, for example, the practice of *dharana*, or concentration, is considered a crucial step towards achieving a state of meditation and inner peace. It is a word that refers to the practice of concentration or focused attention. In Hindu tradition, *dharana* is the sixth limb of yoga and is considered a crucial aspect of spiritual development and self-realization. The word *dharana* is derived from the Sanskrit root '*dhri*' which means 'to hold' or 'to maintain'. *Dharana* is the practice of focusing the mind on a single point, object or thought, and sustaining that concentration without distraction. It is a practice of mental discipline that involves training the mind to be fully present and focused on the task at hand.

The purpose of *dharana* is to prepare the mind for deeper levels of meditation and self-awareness. It is a way of training the mind to be still and focused and to cultivate a sense of inner peace and clarity. Through the practice of *dharana*, one learns to control the fluctuations of the mind and to develop the ability to concentrate deeply and consistently.

In Hindu tradition, *dharana* is often practiced in conjunction with other yogic practices, such as pranayama (breath control) and asana (physical postures). The combination of these practices is designed to help the practitioner achieve a state of inner stillness and tranquility, which is believed to be necessary for spiritual growth and enlightenment. *Dharana* is also considered to be a valuable tool for dealing with the stresses and challenges of everyday life. By learning to focus the mind and maintain concentration, one can develop greater mental clarity, improved decision-making skills, and a greater sense of inner peace and contentment.

Similarly, in Buddhist teachings, the practice of '*samatha*', or calm abiding, involves developing a focused and concentrated mind in order to gain insight into the nature of reality. The practice of *samatha* involves cultivating mindfulness of the breath or a chosen object of focus in order to develop a stable and focused state of mind. This can lead to a sense of mental clarity and calmness, as well as greater awareness and insight.

Samatha meditation is often used as a preparation for other forms of Buddhist meditation, such as vipassana or insight meditation, which involves investigating the nature of reality and developing wisdom.

The development of *samatha* is considered an important aspect of the path to enlightenment in the Buddhist tradition. It is seen as a way to cultivate the mental qualities necessary for deeper understanding and insight, and ultimately liberation from suffering. By calming the mind and developing concentration, the practitioner is able to better understand the nature of their thoughts and emotions and to cultivate a sense of inner peace and well-being.

Scientific research has also demonstrated the benefits of concentration and focus. Studies have shown that practicing mindfulness meditation, which involves cultivating a non-judgmental awareness of the present moment, can lead to improvements in attention, working memory, and cognitive flexibility. Other research has shown that individuals who are able to maintain a high level of focus and concentration are more likely to achieve their goals and experience greater success in their personal and professional lives.

In psychology, the concept of flow is closely related to the idea of one-pointed concentration. Flow is a state of intense focus and absorption in an activity, where the individual feels completely immersed and energized by the task at hand. This state of flow has been linked to greater happiness, creativity, and overall life satisfaction.

Olympic sprinter Usain Bolt, for example, was known for his intense focus and concentration during races, with his ability to block out distractions and maintain his mental composure being key to his success. Similarly, business magnate Warren

Buffet has credited his success to his ability to maintain a focused and disciplined approach to investing, even in the face of marked fluctuations and uncertainty.

The quote 'Whatever you do, do it with one-pointed concentration' highlights the importance of focus and concentration in achieving our goals and living a fulfilling life. By cultivating our ability to concentrate and direct our attention towards the task at hand, we can achieve a greater sense of purpose and meaning in our lives, while also experiencing greater success and fulfilment in our personal and professional endeavors.

❑

32
In the End, Only Three Things Matter

Love, kindness & detachment.

In the end, only three things matter: how much you loved, how gently you lived, and how gracefully you let go of things not meant for you.

—The Buddha

This statement is a beautiful reminder that life is about more than material success or personal achievement. It suggests that, ultimately, what truly matters is how we treat ourselves, others, and the world around us.

One way to approach this statement is to break it down into its three parts and explore each one in more depth. Let us begin with the first part, 'How much you loved'. Love is one of the most powerful human emotions, and it can take many different forms—love for our family, friends, romantic partners, pets, or even love for the world around us. Loving deeply and authentically is an important part of a fulfilling life, and it can have positive impacts on our mental and physical health. Research has shown that people who experience more love and positive emotions in their lives tend to have lower levels of stress, better immune function, and better overall well-being. Love is often described as one of the most powerful emotions and motivators, capable of transcending differences and connecting people across cultures and backgrounds.

Loving relationships have been shown to have numerous benefits for our physical and mental health. For example, studies have found that people in loving relationships tend to have lower levels of stress and anxiety, as well as better cardiovascular health and immune function. Love and positive social connections also help to promote feelings of happiness and well-being.

In addition to romantic love, it's also important to cultivate a sense of love and compassion towards all living beings, including ourselves. Self-love and self-compassion are essential for maintaining a healthy self-image and for building resilience in the face of challenges and setbacks.

Moreover, love and kindness towards others can have a positive ripple effect in the world. When we act with love and compassion, we inspire others to do the same, creating a virtuous cycle of positivity and kindness.

Moving on to the second part, 'How gently you lived', this suggests that we should strive to live our lives with a sense of compassion and kindness towards ourselves and others. It encourages us to approach life with a soft touch, to be mindful of our actions, and to try to do as little harm as possible. Living gently can also mean being present in the moment, taking time to appreciate the beauty around us, and cultivating a sense of gratitude for the small things in life. Living gently means being aware of the impact one's actions have on others and taking steps to minimize harm. It means being mindful of the environment and taking care not to waste resources or pollute the planet. It also means treating oneself and others with kindness and compassion, recognizing that we all have struggles and challenges.

Living gently also involves being present in the moment and finding joy in the simple things in life. It means taking time to appreciate the beauty of nature, spending quality time with loved ones, and cultivating a sense of gratitude for what one has.

By living gently, we can create a more peaceful and harmonious world. When we treat others with kindness and respect, we are more likely to receive the same in return. When we take care of the planet, we can ensure that future generations will have a healthy and thriving environment to live in.

In addition to the benefits to others and the world, living gently can also have a positive impact on our own well-being. When we practice kindness and compassion towards ourselves and others, we can reduce stress, improve our relationships, and increase our overall sense of happiness and fulfilment.

Finally, the third part of the statement, 'How gracefully you let go of things not meant for you', is perhaps the most challenging but also the most important. Letting go can be difficult, especially when we become attached to people, things or ideas. But when we hold onto things too tightly, it can create suffering and prevent us from moving forward. Learning to let go gracefully means accepting what is, even if it is not what we had hoped for, and having the courage to move on and create space for new opportunities and experiences.

Several strategies can help cultivate the ability to let go gracefully. These include:

1. Practice mindfulness: Mindfulness is the practice of being present and non-judgmental in the moment. By developing a regular mindfulness practice, we can become more aware of our thoughts and emotions, allowing us to recognize when we are holding on to something that no longer serves us.

2. Focus on the present moment: When we let go of the past and the future, we are better able to focus on the present moment. This can be done through practices like meditation or simply taking a few deep breaths and grounding ourselves in the present.
3. Practice self-compassion: Letting go can be painful, and it is important to be gentle with ourselves during this process. Practicing self-compassion can help us feel more accepting and supportive of ourselves as we navigate difficult emotions.
4. Set healthy boundaries: Letting go often involves setting healthy boundaries in relationships and other areas of our lives. This can involve saying no to requests that do not align with our values or goals or simply prioritizing self-care.

In terms of ancient wisdom and philosophy, many religious and spiritual traditions emphasize the importance of love, compassion, and letting go. In Buddhism, for example, the concept of impermanence teaches that everything in life is constantly changing and that holding onto anything too tightly will ultimately lead to suffering. The practice of mindfulness and meditation can help us to cultivate a sense of non-attachment and acceptance.

'In the end, only three things matter: how much you loved, how gently you lived, and how gracefully you let go of things not meant for you' is a powerful reminder of what is truly important in life. By focusing on love, compassion, and letting go, we can cultivate a sense of inner peace and happiness, and make a positive impact on those around us.

❑

33
Accept Yourself and Stand on Your Two Feet

It all begins with self-awareness & acceptance.

The most important point is to accept yourself and stand on your two feet.

—Shunryu Suzuki

"The concept of self-acceptance has been discussed and written about for centuries. It is a fundamental aspect of self-help and personal growth. In the words of Daisaku Ikeda, "The most important point is to accept yourself and stand on your two feet." First and foremost, it is important to recognize that self-acceptance is not the same as complacency. Accepting yourself does not mean you are content with your current situation or you are not striving for improvement. It simply means that you acknowledge who you are, with all of your strengths and weaknesses, and that you are willing to work with what you have in order to achieve your goals. This is a vital step towards personal growth and self-improvement.

The concept of standing on your own two feet is closely related to self-acceptance. It is about being independent and self-reliant, and not relying on others to define your sense of self-worth. When you stand on your own two feet, you take responsibility for your own life and your own decisions. You do not allow others to dictate how you should live your life, and you do not depend on them for your happiness.

One of the main benefits of self-acceptance and standing on your own two feet is that it leads to greater self-confidence. When you accept yourself for who you are, you are less likely to be negatively impacted by the opinions of others. You are more likely to have a strong sense of self-worth and less likely to compare yourself to others. Similarly, when you stand on your own two feet, you are less likely to be swayed by external pressures or expectations.

There are many ways to cultivate self-acceptance and stand on your own two feet. One important step is to practice self-compassion. This means treating yourself with kindness and understanding, and recognizing that everyone makes mistakes. Another important step is to focus on your strengths and accomplishments, rather than your weaknesses and failures. By doing so, you can develop a more positive sense of self-worth.

Mindfulness meditation is another powerful tool for cultivating self-acceptance and standing on your own two feet. By practicing mindfulness, you can become more aware of your thoughts and feelings, and learn to accept them without judgment. This can help you to develop a greater sense of self-awareness and self-compassion.

Philosophical and spiritual teachings can also be helpful in cultivating self-acceptance and standing on your own two feet. For example, the ancient Greek philosophy of Stoicism emphasizes the importance of accepting what is outside of your control, and focusing on what is within your control. Similarly, Buddhist teachings emphasize the importance of letting go of attachment and embracing impermanence.

Oprah Winfrey has spoken openly about her struggles with weight and self-esteem, and how she learned to accept herself for who she is. Similarly, Nelson Mandela's ability to forgive his captors and embrace a spirit of reconciliation is a testament to his strength and self-acceptance.

The words of Daisaku Ikeda are a powerful reminder of the importance of self-acceptance and standing on your own two feet. By accepting yourself for who you are, and taking responsibility for your own life, you can develop greater self-confidence and self-worth. By cultivating these qualities through practices like self-compassion, mindfulness, and philosophical and spiritual teachings, you can live a more fulfilling and authentic life.

❑

34
You must be the Change You Wish

Change begins within.

You must be the change you wish to see in the world.
— Mahatma Gandhi

"You must be the change you wish to see in the world" is a powerful statement that has inspired people for generations. It is a call to action, to take responsibility for creating the world we want to live in, rather than waiting for someone else to do it for us. This statement is inspired by ancient Buddhist wisdom and is often attributed to Mahatma Gandhi, one of the greatest leaders of our time, who embodied the values of non-violence, compassion, and social justice.

From Buddhism to Stoicism to modern-day self-help books, the message is clear: true transformation starts with the individual.

The concept of inner transformation is rooted in the idea that our external reality is a reflection of our inner state. This means that if we want to create positive change in the world, we first need to focus on our own thoughts, emotions, and actions. In other words, we need to work on ourselves before we can effectively work on the world around us.

To truly be the change we wish to see in the world, we must start by looking inward. This requires self-reflection, self-awareness, and a willingness to examine our own beliefs, biases, and behaviors. We must be honest with ourselves about our strengths and weaknesses, and be willing to work on improving ourselves.

In ancient wisdom, this principle of self-improvement and self-mastery is central to many spiritual traditions, including Buddhism, Taoism and Stoicism. These teachings emphasize the importance of cultivating inner peace, wisdom and compassion, as a foundation for creating positive change in the world. Buddhism, for example, emphasizes the importance of cultivating inner peace and wisdom through meditation and self-reflection. The Buddha taught that by understanding and transforming our own minds, we can achieve lasting happiness and contribute to the well-being of others. The concept of 'Bodhisattva', a being who is committed to helping others attain enlightenment, embodies this idea of inner transformation leading to a positive impact in the world.

One of the challenges of being the change we wish to see in the world is overcoming our own inertia and taking action. It is easy to feel overwhelmed by the problems of the world or to believe that our individual actions will not make a difference.

The Stoics, a school of philosophy in ancient Greece and Rome, also emphasised the importance of inner transformation.

They believed that by cultivating virtue and wisdom, individuals could achieve a state of inner tranquility and resilience in the face of external challenges. This, in turn, would allow them to make a positive impact in their communities.

Modern-day self-help books and motivational speakers often echo these ancient teachings. They encourage individuals to focus on developing their own strengths and overcoming their weaknesses, with the belief that this will lead to greater success and happiness in all areas of life.

In today's world, many pressing issues demand our attention and action, from climate change to social inequality to political unrest. While it can be tempting to focus all our energy on external problems, it is important to remember that lasting change starts from within.

By working on ourselves, we can become more empathetic, compassionate and effective agents of change. We can cultivate the skills and qualities needed to address the challenges facing our world, such as critical thinking, creativity and resilience. Ultimately, by prioritizing our own inner growth, we can make a positive impact on the world and inspire others to do the same.

The life of Mahatma Gandhi himself is a powerful example of the impact one person can make through their actions. Through his commitment to non-violent resistance, he inspired millions of people to join him in the struggle for Indian independence, and his legacy continues to inspire social justice movements around the world today.

Scientific research also supports the idea that personal transformation is a key component of creating a better world. Studies have shown that mindfulness and self-compassion practices can lead to increased well-being, reduced stress, and improved relationships. These benefits can have a ripple effect, spreading positivity to others around us and inspiring them to make positive changes in their own lives.

Being the change we wish to see in the world requires a commitment to personal growth, self-reflection, and taking action. We must be willing to examine our own beliefs and behaviours, overcome our own inertia, and take steps toward creating a better world. Through our personal transformation, we can inspire others to do the same, creating a ripple effect that can ultimately lead to a more just, compassionate and peaceful world.

"You must be the change you wish to see in the world" is a powerful statement that has inspired people for generations. It is a call to action, to take responsibility for creating the world we want to live in, rather than waiting for someone else to do it for us. This statement is inspired by ancient Buddhist wisdom and is often attributed to Mahatma Gandhi, one of the greatest leaders of our time, who embodied the values of non-violence, compassion, and social justice.

From Buddhism to Stoicism to modern-day self-help books, the message is clear: true transformation starts with the individual.

The concept of inner transformation is rooted in the idea that our external reality is a reflection of our inner state. This means that if we want to create positive change in the world, we first need to focus on our own thoughts, emotions, and actions. In other words, we need to work on ourselves before we can effectively work on the world around us.

To truly be the change we wish to see in the world, we must start by looking inward. This requires self-reflection, self-awareness, and a willingness to examine our own beliefs, biases, and behaviors. We must be honest with ourselves about our strengths and weaknesses, and be willing to work on improving ourselves.

In ancient wisdom, this principle of self-improvement and self-mastery is central to many spiritual traditions, including Buddhism, Taoism and Stoicism. These teachings emphasize the importance of cultivating inner peace, wisdom and compassion, as a foundation for creating positive change in the world. Buddhism, for example, emphasizes the importance of cultivating inner peace and wisdom through meditation and self-reflection. The Buddha taught that by understanding and transforming our own minds, we can achieve lasting happiness and contribute to the well-being of others. The concept of 'Bodhisattva', a being who is committed to helping others attain enlightenment, embodies this idea of inner transformation leading to a positive impact in the world.

One of the challenges of being the change we wish to see in the world is overcoming our own inertia and taking action. It is easy to feel overwhelmed by the problems of the world or to believe that our individual actions will not make a difference.

The Stoics, a school of philosophy in ancient Greece and Rome, also emphasised the importance of inner transformation. They believed that by cultivating virtue and wisdom, individuals could achieve a state of inner tranquility and resilience in the face of external challenges. This, in turn, would allow them to make a positive impact in their communities.

Modern-day self-help books and motivational speakers often echo these ancient teachings. They encourage individuals to focus on developing their own strengths and overcoming their weaknesses, with the belief that this will lead to greater success and happiness in all areas of life.

In today's world, many pressing issues demand our attention and action, from climate change to social inequality to political unrest. While it can be tempting to focus all our energy on external problems, it is important to remember that lasting change starts from within.

By working on ourselves, we can become more empathetic, compassionate and effective agents of change. We can cultivate the skills and qualities needed to address the challenges facing our world, such as critical thinking, creativity and resilience. Ultimately, by prioritizing our own inner growth, we can make a positive impact on the world and inspire others to do the same.

The life of Mahatma Gandhi himself is a powerful example of the impact one person can make through their actions. Through his commitment to non-violent resistance, he inspired millions of people to join him in the struggle for Indian independence, and his legacy continues to inspire social justice movements around the world today.

Scientific research also supports the idea that personal transformation is a key component of creating a better world. Studies have shown that mindfulness and self-compassion practices can lead to increased well-being, reduced stress, and improved relationships. These benefits can have a ripple effect, spreading positivity to others around us and inspiring them to make positive changes in their own lives.

Being the change we wish to see in the world requires a commitment to personal growth, self-reflection, and taking action. We must be willing to examine our own beliefs and behaviours, overcome our own inertia, and take steps toward creating a better world. Through our personal transformation, we can inspire others to do the same, creating a ripple effect that can ultimately lead to a more just, compassionate and peaceful world.

❑

35

The Purpose of Our Lives is to be Happy

Finding & spreading happiness is our true purpose.

The purpose of our lives is to be happy.

—The Dalai Lama

This is a profound statement that has been reiterated by many great thinkers throughout history. It is a simple yet powerful truth that is often forgotten amid our busy lives, distractions, and pursuits of material possessions. In this article, we will explore the idea of happiness as the ultimate goal of human existence and what it means to be truly happy.

Ancient wisdom has long emphasised the importance of inner peace and happiness. The ancient Greeks believed that happiness was the ultimate goal of human existence, and the teachings of Buddhism, Taoism and Hinduism similarly emphasize the importance of inner contentment and peace. For example, the Dalai Lama, a revered spiritual leader and teacher of Tibetan Buddhism, has stated time and again that the sole purpose of our existence and this life we lead is to find and spread happiness.

Scientific research also supports the idea that happiness is a crucial component of human well-being. Studies have shown that people who report higher levels of happiness tend to have better physical health, greater longevity, stronger relationships, and more success in their careers. In addition, happiness has been linked to increased creativity, improved problem-solving abilities, and better decision-making skills.

Psychology also provides insights into the nature of happiness. Positive psychology, a relatively new branch of psychology, focuses on the study of happiness and well-being. It emphasizes the importance of cultivating positive emotions, engaging in meaningful activities, building strong relationships, and finding a sense of purpose in life. Positive psychology research suggests that happiness is not merely the absence of negative emotions, but rather a state of well-being that involves feeling satisfied, fulfilled, and content with one's life.

Philosophy also sheds light on the nature of happiness. Philosophers throughout history have debated the nature of happiness and its relationship to other virtues such as wisdom, courage and justice. Aristotle, for example, believed that happiness was the ultimate goal of human life and that it could be achieved by living a virtuous life. Similarly, Epicurus believed that happiness could be attained by living a simple life and cultivating meaningful relationships with others.

Famous people throughout history have also emphasised the importance of happiness. Mahatma Gandhi, the Indian nationalist leader, once said, "Happiness is when what you think, what you say, and what you do are in harmony." Albert Schweitzer, the Nobel Peace Prize laureate, believed that 'the only true happiness comes from making others happy'. And the renowned scientist, Albert Einstein, once wrote that 'a calm and modest life brings more happiness than the pursuit of success combined with constant restlessness'.

So, what does it mean to be truly happy? While there is no single definition of happiness, some common themes emerge from the above sources. Happiness involves feeling satisfied and content with one's life, having meaningful relationships with others, engaging in activities that bring joy and fulfilment, and having a sense of purpose or meaning in life. It also involves being in harmony with oneself and with the world around us and having a sense of inner peace and contentment.

To achieve happiness, it is important to focus on cultivating positive emotions, engaging in meaningful activities, building strong relationships, and finding a sense of purpose or meaning in life. This can involve practicing gratitude, mindfulness and self-care, as well as pursuing hobbies and interests that bring joy and fulfilment. It also involves cultivating positive relationships with others, showing kindness and compassion to oneself and others, and finding ways to make a positive impact on the world.

In conclusion, the purpose of our lives is to be happy. This idea is supported by ancient wisdom, scientific research, psychology, philosophy, and the examples of famous people throughout history. To be truly happy, it is important to focus on cultivating positive emotions, engaging in meaningful activities, building strong relationships, and finding a sense of purpose or meaning in life.

❑